# NOTHING BUT
# BLUE

# NOTHING BUT
# BLUE

## LISA JAHN-CLOUGH

Houghton Mifflin
Houghton Mifflin Harcourt
Boston   New York   2013

Houghton Mifflin is an imprint of Houghton Mifflin Harcourt Publishing Company.

www.hmhbooks.com

The text of this book is set in Adobe Garamond Pro.

*Library of Congress Cataloging-in-Publication Data*

Jahn-Clough, Lisa.
Nothing but Blue / by Lisa Jahn-Clough.
p. cm.
Summary: Aided by a mysterious, possibly magical dog named Shadow and by various strangers, a seventeen-year-old with acute memory loss who calls herself Blue makes a 500-mile trek to her childhood home, unaware of what she has left behind.
ISBN 978-0-618-95961-7
[1. Amnesia—Fiction. 2. Voyages and travels—Fiction. 3. Dogs—Fiction. 4. Human-animal relationships—Fiction. 5. Homeless persons—Fiction. 6. Death—Fiction. 7. Moving, Household—Fiction.] I. Title.
PZ7.J153536Not 2013
[Fic]—dc23
2012026971

Manufactured in the United States of America
DOC 10 9 8 7 6 5 4 3 2 1
4500404352

Know the universe itself as a road,
as many roads, as roads for traveling souls.

—Walt Whitman

# Now

*All dead. No one survived. All dead.*

The words pound in my head like mini explosions going off again and again and again.

*All dead.* Boom!

*No one survived.* Boom!

*All dead.* Boom!

I don't know what these words mean. I am not dead. I am here, so I have survived. The heavy fog dampens my clothes so that my cutoffs cling to my thighs. I touch the air gingerly, then grab at it as though I can hold on. I rub my fingertips together. They are wet and clammy from the humidity. I feel, therefore I must exist.

I'm not sure where I am. I've been walking since morning, so I must be miles from wherever I began. It's afternoon now.

I find a plot of grass and a tree to lean against. The bark is rough and hard on my back, but it's solid. I flip off my flip-flops and massage one foot, then the other.

I check my pockets. Maybe there's something useful tucked

away. I take out a door key on a mini-flashlight key chain. I blink the beam once, twice, three times and swirl the white light. I can barely see the glow in the misty air.

In the other pocket is a roll of Life Savers. I am suddenly aware that I have not eaten all day. I pop one into my mouth, then two more. I am about to take another when I think perhaps I should save the rest. I fold over the foil wrapper and seal it down with my thumb.

I turn the Life Savers around with my tongue and suck out the sweet juicy flavor to make them last longer. I long for a candy bar, something with hard, dark chocolate outside and gooey, chewy, sweet caramel inside.

The sky darkens under a cloud and the wind blows. It looks like it's going to rain, maybe storm. The days are getting shorter. School will start soon. It will be my last year of high school, but I don't think I'll be going now. I can't shake the feeling that something absolutely awful has happened.

One fat droplet splats on the top of my head. Expecting a downpour, I pull up the hood of my sweatshirt, but there is only that one drop. I'm glad to have the sweatshirt though. I think hard. I try to remember. I almost didn't take it with me. I grabbed it off the chair on my way out the door. It was early in the morning. Was that this morning? What was it I had to get? A cup of coffee? I never got it. I forgot the money. I was going back to get some, and that's it.

Now I don't have the coffee and I don't have the money and I don't know what happened.

*Boom! Boom! Boom!* throbs my brain with the struggle to remember. I beat my palms on my forehead. The exploding will stop if I can just stop thinking.

I search deeper in my pockets. Maybe there's some cash. I do that sometimes, fold up a bill and stick it in my pocket, then forget about it until I next wear the pants and find it all washed and crumpled. I turn the front pockets inside out. Not even a coin—nothing but lint.

So this is what I have:

- half a roll of Life Savers
- one front-door key (useless)
- one flashlight key chain

That's it. That's all she wrote. No more. No less. Once I had everything, and now, *nada*. No money, no phone, no music, no food, no clothes—well, except for the clothes on my back: sweatshirt, T-shirt, cutoffs, flip-flops, underwear. Hard to believe I could be so stupid as to take so little, but I was only going for a few minutes, or so I thought.

I hear my mother's voice somewhere in my head: You're going out in *that?*

And my father: You really should wear better shoes.

Mother: You just don't have the legs for such short shorts, dear.

Father: I don't see how you can walk in those. There's no support.

Mother: At least brush your hair.

Father: We just want what's good for you.

Mother: We just want you to be a normal, happy, pretty girl . . .

Did they actually say these things, or am I imagining things they might say? They always said they just wanted me to be happy. Do they even know I'm gone?

Where are they?

Where am I?

*All dead. No one survived. All dead.*

My throat tightens and my stomach twists into knots. It's hard to breathe. I squeeze my eyes shut. There is a smell that makes me want to vomit. Burning. Smoke. Ash. I gasp for air.

I try to focus on the moment by counting breaths. *One. Two. Three. Four. Five. Six.* I inhale deeper with each count, and the chant grows quieter. By the time I get all the way to fifty it is so faint I can barely hear it. The stench disappears and my stomach loosens. I can swallow.

As I listen to my breath, I stare at an ant on the ground. It's a tiny little thing carrying a crumb twice its size, trudging through grass and over dirt. Suddenly it runs into a twig, and instead of going around, it attempts to climb over without dropping its precious load. The poor little ant is all by itself in a world much larger than it will ever know. I move the twig out of its way, and the ant keeps going as though the twig had never even been there.

I make a pledge to myself—I won't think of anything except what is in front of me. It is the only way. I have no future. I have no past. All I have is now—the clothes on my back, the raindrop on my head, the grass under my feet, the tree pressing against my spine, the woods on either side of me, and the long stretch of road ahead disappearing into a bank of gray fog.

I'm walking along the side of the road with my hood pulled over my face so no one can see me. The air is dark and heavy. My feet ache from the stupid flip-flops. I might as well be barefoot.

My stomach grumbles. I finished off the Life Savers hours ago. So much for saving. I imagine all the things I could eat: a bagel oozing out cream cheese, extra-cheesy pizza, stringy mozzarella sticks, fried chicken fingers, a burger with loads of ketchup, french fries, potato chips, a mocha milk shake, a thick slice of chocolate cake for dessert. I lick my lips.

The rumbling of a pickup truck interrupts my food fantasy. I try to breathe normally even though inside I am trembling. My instincts tell me I shouldn't be "found." The truck comes up behind me. I stare straight ahead.

*It will pass. It will not notice me. It will pass,* I tell myself, like a mantra that will make it true. But it doesn't work. The truck slows to my pace and drives alongside me. I keep walking. *It will pass. It will pass.*

The window rolls down and a guy calls out, "Want a lift?"

I don't dare look, but I imagine a cliché truck guy: cigarette dangling from his mouth, the rest of the pack rolled in the sleeve of his T-shirt, a big grin revealing missing teeth, and some empty beer cans strewn about the front seat.

I shake my head ever so slightly, no, and keep walking straight ahead. My flip-flops slap at my heels with each step.

"You sure? It can be dangerous walking all alone. It's gonna be dark soon," the man says.

This is what every child is warned about. Never trust strange men who sound friendly. Especially men in trucks who offer rides. I make a mistake and glance at him. He is muscular and good-looking and wearing a T-shirt, but there's no cigarette. He smiles wide, and as far as I can tell he has all his teeth.

He asks, "You from around here?"

*Say nothing.*

"Where are you headed?"

*Keep walking.*

He stops the truck. "Hey," he says as he opens the door and steps out.

Everything in me panics. Now I know he is dangerous. He is planning to pick me up, leave me battered on the street, or worse. As he walks around the front of the truck I burst into a run, my shoes flopping and flailing. I have to get away from him. Fast. He yells something about calling for help, something about people looking for me, but I concentrate on running.

A sound echoes somewhere—a single, short bark, then another and another, like a beckoning call. It's coming from the woods. Of course, stupid me. Why am I running straight down the road where he can easily catch me, when I should run where it's harder to follow and easier to hide? I turn and head into the trees toward the barking.

The flower part of one of my flip-flops breaks, and the toe thong pulls out of the sole. I kick both shoes off and keep running. I ignore the sticks and twigs and rocks stinging my bare feet. I pray that the man has not followed me into the woods, but I don't dare stop to find out.

I hear another bark and can make out the dark shadow of an animal in between the trees way ahead. It stands there for a second like it's looking back at me, then takes off at a gallop and disappears into the depths of the forest.

. . .

I've been trudging slowly along and now it is quickly darkening into night. There's not much along this road; it is straight and rural with a lot of cornfields. I stop at the next building I come to —a brick restaurant with a sign on the roof that reads FIREFLY in hot red letters. Under that is says: HOME-COOKED BREAKFAST AND LUNCH.

I am dying for something to eat and drink. Although dying may be an exaggeration. Funny how we use that expression so easily. Am I dying? Am I dead already?

*All dead, all dead, all dead. No one survived.* The words become a steady chant again, but this time I am better able to ignore them, since the grumbling of my stomach is even stronger.

I sit by the side of the building and cradle my tender feet. I've stubbed my toes more than once, and one of them is caked with blood. I spit on my finger and try to wash it off, but it smears a muddy, bloody streak across my foot.

A street lamp flickers and buzzes out. It is really dark now— there is no moon or stars. Tears burn in my eyes but I cannot cry. There's nothing to cry about—this is just the way it is now.

Next to me are a couple of dumpsters. I bet there's leftover food in there. I crawl over and peer inside the closest one. It's all recycling—nothing but paper and cardboard. I go to the other. I shine the flashlight key chain into the foul depths.

The dumpster is full of black garbage bags, rotten food, Styrofoam containers, and other unidentifiable trash. The smell makes me want to puke. I snatch one of the containers and move away.

The container is half full of spaghetti soaked in red sauce with part of a meatball perched on the top. I poke the meatball with my finger. It's mushy and totally gross. I can't eat someone's old leftover, thrown-out spaghetti dinner. This will make me sick for sure. Is it better to die of starvation or food poisoning? I place the box next to me. My stomach begs to be fed, but I'm not ready to eat garbage. Not yet.

I lie down on the hard, damp pavement. I close my eyes. I feel . . . nothing. I see . . . nothing. The chant is a buzz of white noise in the dark.

Then out of the blackness comes a vision of smoldering rubble, crumpled piles of wood, brick, rock—it looks like a war zone. The insanity of fire trucks, police, ambulance, neighbors screaming. That stench of smoke fills my nostrils again and dries my throat, as though the ash has crawled deep inside.

I hear words. This time they are not a chant but clear single words, one at a time: *Explosion . . . Leak . . . Inside . . . Dead . . . Impossible . . . No, possible.*

I see these images, I hear these words, but when I open my eyes all I see is the black pavement, the brick wall; everything else is just night. The street lamp hums and flickers on again, blazing the letters of the restaurant sign in red flashes. FIREFLY. FIREFLY. Moths hover around the sudden light and ding into it. The moon emerges from behind the clouds. A few stars blink. The nightmare images have nothing to do with me; my mind is playing tricks.

This is what is real: I'm freezing. I'm starving. I'm tired. I'm in pain. There is no way I can sleep like this. I need something to lie on and something to cover me.

Still shaking, I get up and go over to the recycle dumpster. I take out some of the larger boxes. I arrange them along the wall of the restaurant. I line the ground with the flat pieces, then make walls and a roof. I crawl inside and prop another piece against the opening, leaving a tiny crack.

It's dark and musty, but I'm somewhat proud of my cave—like the pillow tents I made when I was little. No one could find me under a mound of pillows.

This time when I lie down it's on a cardboard mat. At least it's better than the pavement. I shut my eyes again and try to shut my mind at the same time. I breathe in through my mouth and out through my nose like they tell you in yoga. Or is it in the nose and out the mouth? I never can remember.

*Breathe in. Count to ten. Breathe out. In. Count. Out. In. Count. Out.*

Now all I smell is damp cardboard. All I hear are a few raindrops pittering on the roof. The rest drifts away. I am shut tight in this box, safe for the moment.

But not for long. Suddenly the quiet is interrupted by a scratching sound on the outside of my shelter, like fingernails. Immediately I think, *Police—they found me.* Didn't that man in the truck say people are looking for me?

A police officer would probably take me back. But back where? I can't go back to nothing. I brace myself and prepare for an intruder. But the sound has stopped and all is still and quiet again. Did I imagine it, like everything else?

What would I tell a cop? I'm supposed to start my senior year. These are supposed to be the best years of my life, but I know they are not. The only things I remember clearly are from long ago, like where I was born, the sound of gulls in the morning, and the smell of the ocean coming through the window. I remember being a little girl. I remember painting a mural of trees on my bedroom wall. I remember my mother and father. They want what's best for me, but how do they know what is best for me when I don't have a clue?

And then I remember Jake. He gave me a bracelet. I look at my wrist. I am still wearing it—it's an embroidery rope of all different colors. I run my finger along the silklike braid. Jake was real. Jake meant something.

But how did I get from there to here? I'm not anywhere near the ocean—there are forests and fields all around; nothing is familiar.

There is the scritching sound again, followed by a whimper. It's some kind of animal—could be a raccoon or a skunk. I've heard raccoons can be vicious, and I don't relish the idea of skunk spray, so I stay very still.

Then, thumping on the side of the box and a shiny black nose pokes through the opening. The nose belongs to a dog. A damp, dirty, smelly dog.

"Shoo," I say. It doesn't come any closer, but its tail goes wild, *whomp, whomp, whomp*ing against the heavy cardboard. "Go on, get out of here." I try to wave it away.

But the dog doesn't listen. It noses in the rest of the way and sniffs. It has dark-gray mottled fur and flecks of white on its long, skinny tail. Its ears are alarmingly tall and point straight up. Its whole body wags like crazy. He is small enough to fit in the box with me but too big to be a lap dog.

I can tell by the way he lifts his head toward me that he wants me to touch him. His fur is matted and he needs a bath. I am afraid he might have fleas and who knows what else. I hold my hands away.

"Don't come any closer," I say.

He keeps sniffing around like he's looking for something. His eyes rest on the Styrofoam container I'd tossed in the corner. Of course, he's attracted to the smell of the rotten, leftover spaghetti.

"Is this what you want?" I hand him the box. "Go ahead, I'm not eating this crap." As I say it my stomach growls. The dog hesitates a second, then takes the container in his mouth and slowly backs out the way he nosed in.

# Before

I thought romance would never happen to me, that somehow I had whatever it was that made me totally unnoticeable to anyone. I had pretty much given up on the idea of love. But then something happened.

It was a white-hot afternoon—unheard of, even for July. There was nothing to do, so I figured I'd buy an ice cream cone and go to the town beach. I made it halfway down the driveway before turning into a torrent of sweat. I had to lie down on the grass and close my eyes. The sun seared through my lids. The music pulsed through my headphones.

All of a sudden I felt movement. I opened my eyes to a pair of sneakers next to my head. I shaded the sun with my hand and kept my eyes going up. There were strong muscled calves covered with soft golden hairs, surfer shorts, and arms folded across his crisp white T-shirt. He was backlit, so I couldn't quite see his face, but I could tell he had short hair, slicked back. I thought it must take a lot of effort to get hair so smooth like that.

He moved to one side, out of the sun. He looked familiar, but I couldn't quite place how. He grinned down at me with perfectly straight teeth and waved. Now I recognized him. It was Jake, the towheaded rich boy who lived in the fancy McMansion at the end of the street. His hair had darkened into copper, and I swear he was at least a foot taller than the last time I saw him. He was hardly a boy anymore. Can someone grow that much in such a short time? He'd only left for prep school last fall.

His mouth moved in the shape of words. I pulled out an ear-bud. Tinny music filled the air.

"What're you doing?" he asked.

"What does it look like I'm doing?"

"It looks like you're lying in the middle of the lawn. I thought maybe you were dead. I came over to check." His smile grew, so I figured he was kidding.

"Oh," I said. Suddenly I was nervous; I wanted to say the right thing, but I wasn't sure what that was.

"Guess you're not dead," he said.

I smiled meekly and shook my head. "Guess not."

When we were little all the kids hung out at Jake's house. Mainly because he had a swimming pool and his parents didn't pay attention. I went but he never noticed me. Until one day out of the blue, he handed me a bouquet of dandelions and asked me to marry him. We were eight.

The dandelions were bright yellow—they didn't seem like weeds at all. When I said yes, he hit me with his swim noodle and said he was just kidding. He swam back to his friends, who laughed and started singing the kissing song. I heard them all the way down the street as I ran home.

I cried to my mother. She said that's what boys do and that I should avoid being alone with them from now on. I tried to resurrect the soaked dandelions in a vase, but they were too limp. My mother threw them out.

After that I stopped going over there. Eventually everyone split into cliques and I wasn't in his, or any, for that matter. Jake became the leader of the cool kids, and I became nothing. Then last year his parents sent him away to prep school. He'd looked exactly the same when he left as he did when he was eight—a goofy, skinny, blond boy.

But there he was standing over me, all grown up. He'd filled out with muscles and goldenness. He even had facial hair groomed into a goatee.

"They must've put something in your food," I said.

"Huh?" he said.

"You've grown. Must be the nutrition at that school."

"Yeah, something like that." He was still grinning ear to ear. "You've grown, too," he said.

Yeah, I thought to myself, but I'd gotten wider, not taller. Chubbed right out, as my mother constantly reminded me. I knew I could stand to lose a few, but I liked junk food way too much to bother.

"Of course it's hard to tell when you're horizontal." He offered me a hand, but I ignored it and got myself up. I wiped away some loose grass that had stuck to the back of my sweaty legs. I was embarrassed in the ratty gym shorts and dirty T-shirt I'd thrown on. My hair was unwashed, and my whole body was drenched in sweat.

"Lucky I came along and got you out of your stupor," he said. "You were about to become fried egg."

"I'm fine," I said. "I was going to the store, just connecting with nature first."

"I'm not sure I'd call the lawn nature. Or headphones stuck in your ears, either." Even his voice was different. It had deepened into something much more soothing and gentle. He was the same Jake, and yet he was entirely different.

"You have to listen to nature," he said. He swept his arm around as if presenting a show.

I pulled out the other earbud and turned the music off.

We listened together. Every sound was enhanced: A robin twittered, gulls squawked, a car drove by, a sprinkler went on next door. In the distance we heard the soft roar of the ocean's surf as it met the town beach. We turned our heads up at the same time to the one puff of cloud. The cloud seemed to sigh, heavy with its burden of heat. Jake sighed, too. I glanced at him and he glanced back. The air between us zapped electrical currents back and forth. I felt as though something, maybe everything, was going to change.

I swallowed, suddenly parched. "I see what you mean," I said. I had to get away from the intensity of the moment. I pointed to my house. "I need some water," I said.

"Weren't you going somewhere?" he asked.

"Too hot," I said as I turned.

"Wait." He reached to touch my hair. He untangled a twig and handed it to me. "I'm around all summer. Let's hang out sometime."

# Now

"Knock, knock. Who's there?" a voice asks. There is tapping on the side of my cardboard home.

I open my eyes. Sunlight streams through the cracks, making the whole inside glow orange.

"Come on out—no loitering on the property," the voice says.

This is it. I'm a goner.

I lift up the top of my box and see a tubby, middle-aged man standing there. He's wearing a bright blue T-shirt that has the words FIREFLY RESTAURANT in the same red lettering as the sign. If he's surprised to see a barefoot, teenage girl sleeping in a box, he doesn't show it.

"I don't care if you're here at night, but during the day, it looks bad," he says. "We're about to open, and I don't want the customers startled." The man leans a little closer and studies me. "You look familiar." He pauses, scratches his head in concentration. "You look a little like that girl from the news this morning." He shakes his head and makes a clucking sound. "What a tragedy . . . the house . . . and everything . . ."

I want to flee, but my legs are frozen. I get a flashing vision of a house. The taste of ash fills my mouth, the awful images start to appear, and the *all dead* chant starts up again, good and loud.

An ugly, modern house in an ugly neighborhood, but that house . . . that house has nothing to do with me. I suck in air and try to push the images out and replace them with the house I know—the pale yellow two-story Victorian with green shutters. Where I was born. By the sea.

"Are you okay?" the man asks.

My stomach surges. I concentrate on my house. I imagine opening the front door, walking up the curved stairs with the polished wood banister I used to slide down. At the top is my bedroom. This is my house. I don't know any other. This man doesn't know what he's talking about. I swallow. I stammer to get words out. "I'm not . . . I'm not her."

The man looks me straight in the eye. "Yeah, that girl looked way preppy. My mistake." The man glances down at my feet. "What happened to your shoes? Are you a runaway? Do I need to call someone?"

I shake my head and try to breathe. From out of nowhere the dog from last night appears at my side. He stares at me with his black eyes and rotates his pointed ears. He leans into my leg. His weight presses against me and holds me steady. Surprisingly, my nausea subsides. The ash taste is gone.

"Is that your dog?" the man asks. "He was hanging around yesterday, looking for something, but he wouldn't let me come close. I thought he was feral."

The dog puts all his weight onto me. I wiggle my leg to push him away. He moves over an inch and sits.

"What's your name?" I'm not sure if the man is asking me or the dog. He asks again.

I open my mouth. I'm sure I know my name, but I can't say it. I can't tell him. That name is no longer me. That name belongs to some other me. Someone like me, but not me.

I stare at the man's T-shirt. It's the same color as the ocean on a perfect, calm day. I speak and the word that comes out is "Blue."

The man tilts his head in a question. "Blue?"

"Blue," I repeat, nodding.

"Well, Blue," the man says, glancing at my feet again. "Wait here." He goes inside the restaurant.

This is my chance. I'm about to make a break for it, but the dog starts running circles around my legs so I can't leave, and before I know it the man is back and the dog is still again.

The man holds a pair of red Converse sneakers in one hand. "These are my daughter's. You look like you could be the same size." He dangles the shoes in the air like a treat.

Another warning every child knows: Never take candy from strangers.

"Go on. She left them in the restaurant. She has so many shoes she'll never notice."

The dog takes one of the sneakers in his mouth and drops it at my feet. I take the other. I slide them on. Red is not my color and they are a little big but beggars can't be choosers.

In the other hand the man has a wax-paper bag with a brown

muffin in it. "Take this, too. But you have to go. I really can't have loitering."

I take the bag without hesitating, just like candy, and the man goes back inside to open up.

I hold the muffin to my nose and sniff. Food! Real food! The dog quirks his head like he's expecting something.

"Are you crazy?" I say. "I gave you that spaghetti last night. This is mine." It's a carrot-raisin muffin. I hate carrots and I hate raisins, but suddenly they are the best food ever. I scarf the entire muffin in four bites.

The man peers out the window, so I lace up the shoes and start walking. Even though the shoes are too big, they make a huge difference.

The dog sticks to my heels.

I turn and say, "You can't follow me."

He stops.

I walk ahead, though I sense that I'm being watched. I look back and the dog is standing there with sad, confused eyes. Somehow his eyes lure me over. I kneel down to face him. From a distance they look black, but up close his eyes are all different colors: green, brown, yellow, red, purple. The colors swirl and flicker like a fortune-teller's ball. For a second I am lost in them, swimming around in a warm, peaceful sea. I feel calm, as if I'm in another world.

Then, just as quickly, it's over.

"Look," I say, "you have to leave. I gave you that food last night only because I couldn't eat it."

He hangs his head as if he understands what I'm saying. He pulls his mouth back, opens it slightly. I back away, afraid he might bite me. But then the weirdest thing—his mouth turns up at the corners, and he is smiling. A real smile. He nods his head up and down before he turns and walks away. We go in opposite directions.

My mouth is dry. How long can a person go without water? Two days? Three? A week? A month? In school once we watched a film about Gandhi. He starved himself for something like three weeks. He did it for a cause, for peace. But I bet he had water. It's water that you really can't survive without. In the end it wasn't starvation that killed Gandhi. He was shot.

My muscles are sore, and the weird thing is, they hurt even more when I stop. So I keep moving. It's very rural around here, which is good, I guess. The fewer people the better. I pass an occasional farm or hay field dotted with cows and sheep. The cows chew their cuds and stare at me.

*What are you doing out here?* they seem to ask. *What's the hurry? Don't you want to stop and rest awhile?* They are so peaceful standing among the dandelions, but I walk on by without answering.

The day gets foggier and darker. The ground is wet and the road is full of puddles from a recent rain. I try to avoid muddying my sneakers, but I look no more than three yards ahead. Just get me through the next three yards. I can't think beyond that. It's too far in the future.

A car with a muffler missing and music blaring out the windows catches up to me. The bass is so loud that the whole car shakes. It swerves by extra fast through a puddle, spraying me with dirty water. It's a car full of teens—boys and girls—laughing and bouncing like they're on their way to a party. Two of them stick their heads out the window and yell. The music is so loud that I can't make out the words, but it sounds like something unmentionable. One of them gives me the finger. They speed out of sight.

I am left on the side of the road with the echo of the bass ringing in my ears, soaking wet and thirsty. I want to cry, but it seems too stupid and wasteful. I want to remember things, but that seems stupid, too.

The time and the miles go by. I start to pass more buildings — I must be nearing a town of sorts. I walk by a house close to the road where a woman is tending her flower beds. Dare I ask for water? She waves and nods hello and I quicken my pace.

The businesses that I come across are quiet and closed — it must be after five already. There's an RV sales lot, numerous garages with old rusted cars and trucks dotting the grounds, a Laundromat, a hunting and fishing store. The fog lifts and the late sun comes out extra hot. I consider lapping water from a puddle, but I push forward until I finally come to a gas station that is open. I scope it out.

There's a cashier inside. A woman. A car pulls in for gas, and when the driver goes into the store, I slip inside after him. If I follow someone, I'll stand out less.

I find the bathroom in the back. The sink is metal and there is toilet paper strewn about. There is a distinct odor of bodily functions I'd rather not think about. I turn the faucet on. The water comes out the color of rust. It occurs to me that it could be tainted with something carcinogenic. But on the other hand, I may not be around long enough to get cancer, so I lean under the faucet and let the water stream into my mouth. It is warm and tastes like tin. Tin water is better than no water. I take long, deep gulps until I'm quenched.

When I exit, the customer is gone. The cashier looks up, surprised to see me. She's a girl close to my age. "Hey," she says. "Where'd you come from?"

I mumble a few words telling her it's okay, I'm leaving, but I doubt she understands. Luckily I get out without her asking anything else. I can sense her watching me, wondering maybe, but that's all. At least I got water, and I feel a thousand times better.

There's a fire-orange sunset. Everything blazes up and then starts to turn a deep purple. It's hard to see when all of a sudden a dark animal ambles across the road a few yards ahead. At first, I think it's that dog, but it's way too small, more the size of a heavy cat. It's a little more than halfway across when a car comes barreling toward it.

"Run," I shout. Instead the animal sits up on its hind haunches and stares in my direction as if trying to figure out who is yelling. The car headlights glare and I can see its masked face. A raccoon. "Run!" I shout again, but it is frozen. I turn and wave my arms toward the car frantically to get it to slow down, but it doesn't. There's not much of a curb, so I quickly jump into the bushes to avoid being hit.

The raccoon is not so lucky. There's a heavy *ca-thunk*. The car brakes for a second and idles. I see two people inside talking to each other. The driver looks back and then pulls away just as fast. The road is quiet and empty again, except for the lump of fur and bones left in the middle.

I don't know if the raccoon is dead or not. I walk up to it cautiously. It lies on its side. I crouch to see if it's breathing. I don't think it is. Its eyes bug out a little and there's blood and something else oozing out of its middle.

I'm afraid to touch it, but I can't leave it there in the middle of the road. I find a big stick and push it into the woods. It's heavy. It's getting dark, so I try to move quickly. I dig an indentation big enough to roll the raccoon into it.

"I'm sorry," I whisper. I cover the raccoon with dirt and leaves and leave the stick in the ground like a headstone. It all happened so fast. One second the raccoon was alive and now it's not. *They're all dead!* A voice screams inside me.

I stop at the next building—a place that sells tombstones. How fitting. I huddle in the back against the wall and hug myself for warmth.

The second I close my eyes I see the exploding images. I must be hallucinating. Maybe the lack of food and the cold are making me see things like a drug trip. I've heard of that. Before dying you see all sorts of crazy things. When I open my eyes the hallucination is gone.

I twist my hands up inside the sleeves of my sweatshirt and wrap my arms together. The tin water has left a funny taste in my mouth. My tongue is dry and thick. I lie on my side but keep my eyes open.

I watch a shadow move in the distance. Some kind of animal is walking across the road toward me. It is not a raccoon—that I can tell. It looks like a wolf. It's probably another hallucination. There can't be wolves out here. I blink. It's still there. As it gets closer I see it's a dog with something in its mouth.

The dog comes right up to me and sits by my head. It looks exactly like the dog from the restaurant. Could it be? The thing in its mouth is a plastic water bottle. I try to shoo the dog away, but my arm is stuck in my sleeve. He drops the bottle onto the ground, then backs up a few feet. If I could just take my arm out of my sleeve, I could pick up the bottle. I imagine doing it first, and then I actually am doing it.

The bottle is three-quarters full. It must have been someone else's water, but I don't care. I don't care if there are germs. I don't care if someone spit in it. I don't care if the dog lunges after me and bites my hand. I glance at him. He sits, watching me. It is definitely the same dog. He has the same tall ears and gray, mangy fur. I look into his black eyes and see the swirling flecks of color. I manage to half sit up, unscrew the cap, and raise the bottle to my mouth.

The water slides down my insides. I never knew how good real water could taste. It trickles through my body, giving me life. So much better than gas station tin water.

I cough, then take another sip, more slowly this time. I sit up fully. Amazing how something as simple as water can make me feel so much better.

The dog gives out one short bark. I close my eyes and take another drink. I think I can sleep now.

"Thanks," I murmur, but my voice is so distant, I don't know if anything comes out.


The dog is gone when I wake up. The water bottle is at my feet. I drink the remaining drops. It's true I am not dead, but I'm not quite human anymore. I am just a thing, a mechanical robot. All I need is a little oil rubbed into my joints and muscles and I'll be good again. I get up, stretch my sore back, and leave. My stomach is tight and needs fuel as well.

I walk mindless and numb. It's not cold anymore; in fact, now it's hot. This time of year, you never can tell what the weather will do. Cold at night, hot during the day. One minute it's Indian summer; the next there could be frost.

My thoughts are wrapped inside thick fog, even though the sun is bright. Everything has a hazy quality, as if shivering slightly. Perhaps this is what happens to people in the desert. I'm not in the desert, though. I can make out pastures with rolling hills and green hues of grass. There is a lumpy white and black shape in the distance, and another and another, all forming a large mass. I rub my eyes. Cows. Under a tree. I move toward them. Maybe the cows will share their shade with me.

I hasten my pace. I'm afraid that the tree could be a mirage and will disappear if I don't reach it in time. The cows part as I approach, then settle back around, giving me a wide berth. They seem to be waiting. They talk to me like others I've passed, but this time I listen.

*We knew you could make it,* they say. *Come sit, take a load off.*

I sit against the tree. I don't even mind the pasture smell.

The air is instantly cooler under the leaves.

I spot a small yellowish ball on the ground. That's odd. Is it a tennis ball? Who plays tennis in a cow field? I glance around. The ground is littered with them.

I look up. The tree hides more of the balls in its branches. Not tennis balls, apples! This tree bears fruit. Fruit is edible. I pick an apple up from the ground next to me. It's mottled with brown, but I don't care. There's no such thing as a poison apple, unless you're Snow White, which I most definitely am not, so I bite into the fruit. It's sour, bitter, mealy, and completely delicious.

I eat the entire thing, even the core. I eat a second one just as quick. The third one I pick from the tree, and it is even better. I select the best ones now, as many as I can, and make a pile. I sit on the soft, cool earth with my back against the trunk of my glorious apple tree and eat until I can't eat anymore. A couple of cows bellow me a lullaby.

When I awake, the sun has moved to the other side of the sky and the air is considerably more tolerable. The cows have sauntered away to a brighter pasture. I can make them out as little spots on the hillside. I stuff as many apples as I can into the large front pocket of my sweatshirt. I place my palm on the tree in thanks and wave goodbye to the cows even though they can't see me. I make my way back to the road.

The sun is behind me now. My vision is clear. Even my muscles have stopped complaining. They have accepted their fate. I have control over them, at least for the time being. The fruit has fueled me, and I am ready to continue.

The nap has cleared my mind as well. It is nice and empty. I don't think of anything. I don't feel anything except the weight of the apples in my pocket. I remember the ant that just keeps going against all odds. Am I the ant?

The scent of pine wafts over me. Even the grass has a deep smell. My breathing is steady with my movement. I hum a little, but I'm not even conscious of what it is I'm humming. It doesn't matter. I swing my arms and let my feet match the gait. There's no hurry. I will conserve my batteries, move my feet slowly and steadily. Be the ant.

I can't shake the feeling that something is following me. I instinctively keep in the shadows and walk on the edge of the tree line. I'm still not sure where I am going or why I am here, but I am compelled to put one foot in front of the other and move forward. I've never been in shape or cared much about exercise. I imagine I look something like a waddling penguin in bright red sneakers.

My legs feel like old, hard rubber. *Stop, stop, stop!* they scream. *Let us rest.* But I am afraid to stop because if I do, I may never get up again. I tell my legs to shut up and just keep walking, but they don't obey. Instead they take me to a shady spot nearby, and I sit. First my right thigh begins to tingle, then my left, then the sensation jumps to my right knee, and finally migrates around my entire body. It's like my legs are still walking on the inside even though I am motionless on the outside. I knead my calves with my fists, telling my body to calm down. It helps a little. I have one apple left. I eat it.

Every time a car passes, my body tenses. Since the guy in the truck, which was so long ago already, no one has stopped, and I count on the fact that most people don't care about anyone other than themselves. It's an easy world to slip through unnoticed. I've done it all my life already, except maybe once when I felt like I mattered to someone. My mind goes to Jake. Is he waiting for me? Expecting me? I rub my bracelet and get up again.

I walk until it's dark and I come to a sleepy town that is already shut down for the night. I am on a good old-fashioned Main Street. I can see the marquee of an old movie theater at the end of the block. Some letters are missing, so it reads MA N STR ET THEATRE.

I scan the street for a bearable place to lie down. I don't relish another night in a box or on a bench. I pass several antique stores, a hobby shop, an old-time pharmacy, a barber with a real red and white pole, and an Italian bakery. There are back-to-school posters in the windows. On the lawn of the library is a pumpkin patch and a scarecrow. Signs on the shops all say SHOP DOWNTOWN or SUPPORT LOCAL BUSINESS. There is something a bit surreal about this place, as though it's a town that time forgot.

With some luck this town is so old-fashioned that no one bothers to lock anything, but there is no such luck—all the doors I try are bolted. I reach the Ma n Str et Theatre. It looks like they used to actually have live theater here—there are some old, torn posters of *The King and I, Guys and Dolls,* and *The Pajama Game.* But it's all boarded up now. I rattle the chains on the door. Nothing budges. I walk around the side looking for an open window or crawlspace. Nothing. All the windows are nailed shut with wooden boards.

I sigh. I guess it's outdoors once again. I don't know how much more of this I can stand, but then I don't know what other choice I have. I push through some bushes to see if I can find a soft spot of dirt.

There is a rustling in front of me. There is something already in these bushes. I step back. As the shape emerges I see that it is a dog. I shine my flashlight and its eyes are all glittery and glowing. It is *the* dog.

"You," I say. "Why are you following me?"

The dog whimpers and raises his snout. I follow his gaze with the flashlight. On the second floor right above the fire escape is a window that is not boarded up. Part of the glass is smashed.

I look down at the dog. "How did you know?" I ask.

He just sits patiently staring at me with those spooky eyes and giant ears. In spite of myself, I smile. I am starting to think maybe this is not your ordinary mangy mutt.

"You really don't have any better place to go?" I ask.

He gets up and shakes his body, then nods his nose at the fire escape nearby, as if to encourage me to climb it.

"All right, I see it."

I have to stretch my arms to reach the first rung. Bits of rust fall on top of me. I wipe my hands, then try again. The ladder creaks as I hoist myself up. I wait to see if it will hold my weight. It seems okay, so I climb the rest of the way to the window.

The broken part is too small for me to fit through. I jiggle out a piece of the pane and gently place it on the sill. Even though the pane is already broken—some kids goofing around with a ball I'd guess—I don't want it to look like it's been vandalized.

I remove enough of the glass to crawl inside. Before I do I look down, wondering if the dog is climbing after me, and if should I help him. But once again the dog has disappeared.

# Before

Jake called the day after we met, or, rather, re-met.

"There's this thing tonight," he said. "Of my father's. Do you want to come?"

Not the most romantic way to be asked out, but still, a date's a date, even if an unromantic one. I didn't know for sure if Jake was single. There was this girl at school, Adrianna, who used to talk about him like they were an item, but apparently they weren't or else he wouldn't be asking me out, right?

"What kind of thing?" I asked.

"An art opening," he said.

Jake's father owned some kind of high-end art gallery. He auctioned off estate art to superrich people, which in turn made Jake's family superrich. Though it was also said that most of their money was inherited and the art thing was more of a hobby. Either way, they were millionaires several times over.

"I thought you might like it," Jake told me. "You're artsy, right?"

I laughed, feeling like a normal, popular schoolgirl. "I guess."

People thought I was artsy because I always took art electives in school. In truth I sucked at art. I could barely draw a stick figure with a stick. The only artsy thing I'd ever done was paint a mural of trees on my bedroom wall when I was ten. I wanted it to look like the forest out of a fairy tale so fairies would come live with me. I even painted a tiny mushroom-shaped house underneath the trees especially for them.

Still, I signed up for art electives. No one really knew that you don't have to be good at art to be in an art class. As long as I looked like I was engaged in making marks on paper or pushing clay around, the teachers left me alone. Art class was a place where it didn't matter if you were cool or popular or smart or anything. It didn't matter what you were.

"Great, so you'll come?" Jake asked.

"Sure."

We arranged to meet at his house at six forty-five. It was noon. I had six hours and forty-five minutes to find something to wear. I opened my closet. Even my nicest clothes were boring, not artsy at all.

I got my allowance and headed downtown.

I settled on a black dress. Nothing fancy or lacey, not like a cocktail dress or anything, but a long, slightly fitted stretchy material that didn't make me look too fat. It came to just above my knees with a flirty flare and had a tuck in the waist that actually gave me a little shape. There were three tiny buttons at the neck. I bought a light blue camisole to peek out when the buttons were open. It showed some cleavage.

I went home, bathed, and dressed. I felt good. I even thought

I looked pretty good, too. Maybe this look suited me more than my usual baggy, comfort cotton. I left my hair down, slightly mussed. I finished it all off with a necklace with a tiny turquoise stone that rested in my jugular notch.

I tried to tiptoe down the stairs, but of course Mom caught me before I could get past her office.

"Where are you going?" She peered from her desk. "You're all dressed up."

"Out," I said, as if I always went out on Friday evenings.

She got up and stood in the doorway. "Really?" She smiled, suddenly all friendly. "Out? Where?"

"An art opening."

"An art opening?" She was trying to sound casual, but she couldn't hide her excitement. "That sounds like fun. Who with?"

I sighed. She wanted so badly for me to be normal, to have a group of friends, to be all social and upbeat. Like she was. It was sweet in a way, but it wasn't me.

"Some kids from school," I said. I didn't want to tell her it was a date. I especially didn't want to tell her it was Jake. She'd never liked Jake. She wouldn't understand that he had changed. It was easier to let her think what she wanted to think.

And she did. She clasped her hands. "Oh, honey, I'm so glad. See? High school's not so bad after all. But are you sure that's the right thing to wear? Can I just fix your hair a bit?"

"I've got to go. I'll be late."

"Right, right. You go and have fun. Go out after if you want with the group. Just don't eat too much, okay? It's not ladylike to eat in front of others, and you don't want to get fat."

My mother was a social magnet. But she wasn't big on dating

—she thought a group was better. "Gives you a chance to be friends with girls and boys," she had told me numerous times. "Then if you meet someone who might be something more, you'll know them as friends first. That's the best way. You're not ready to get too attached to just one person at your age."

She was wrong about that. I was totally ready to get attached to just one person.

# Now

I wake to the smell of doughnuts. Fresh, warm, scrumptious doughnuts. There are sounds of a town waking up. Delivery trucks. Doors being unlocked. A few good-mornings are called out. The sun stretches through the window and lights up my sleeping spot in the old theater. I couldn't see much last night in the dark and was too tired even to take out my flashlight. I just crawled to a corner and stayed there.

But now I can see that the ceiling beams are full of cobwebs and spiders. Some very large and creepy. Not too far from where I'd slept, the floorboard is so rotted that a hole has eaten through it. It's amazing I didn't fall through.

I stand carefully and stretch. I run my hands through my hair in an attempt to comb it. I don't know why, because it's not like there's anything I can do about it anyway, nor is there anyone to care. Still, I don't want to draw attention to myself by looking like a ratty homeless girl. I lift my arms and sniff. I stink. Not much I can do about that, either.

I ease myself down the fire escape and back into the world for another day.

I find myself standing in front of one of the bakeries with my nose in the air. I remind myself of the dog, and wonder where he came from and where he's gone to now.

"Excuse me," says a woman from behind me. "I'm just opening." She is large, with a wide roll of fat under her chin, the kind of woman you might expect to work in a bakery. She wears a hairnet, and a red and white striped apron peeks out from under her blue jacket, making her look like an American flag.

She jiggles the lock and holds the door open. "You coming in?" She glances at something near my legs. "No dogs, though. He has to stay out."

I spin around and there he is. The dog. I feel a slight twinge of relief at seeing him again. I'm about to explain that he isn't my dog, but instead I shake my head and tell the woman I'm leaving.

She shrugs. "Suit yourself. Our doughnuts are the best. The baker's just about to take out a fresh batch, if you change your mind."

I walk to the end of the block and think of how I can get some food. The dog follows about ten paces behind. I watch the woman put a sign on the sidewalk that announces HOT COFFEE/FRESH DOUGHNUTS. I can almost taste those doughnuts. Even the dog licks his lips. The woman looks at me for a minute as though she wants to say something, but she turns back inside. The door jingles shut behind her.

I go to the alley behind the bakery and look through the garbage bins. There's nothing that looks or smells edible. I thought for sure there'd be some day-old baked goods. I could eat day-olds. Maybe she hasn't gotten rid of them yet. She'll probably throw them out soon and I can go back and get them. I'll have to wait. The dog sniffs around, too, but comes up empty-handed.

I go to the park across the street and sit on a bench in the sun. The dog dutifully sits next to me. I look at him and he looks back.

"I don't have any food," I say.

He raises his paw in the air like a wave hello.

"Why are you following me? What do you want?" I know he can't answer, but I almost wouldn't be surprised if he could. There's definitely something peculiar about him. He wriggles closer and stretches his neck. This time I let his head rub under my palm. He is surprisingly soft for a stray, though my hand is kind of greasy when I take it away.

"You know, all you really need is a bath." I wipe my hand on my shorts. "But then, so do I, so I guess we're even."

There is a strange peace as the dog and I sit together. It's too early for shoppers. Most things don't open until ten, and I'll be long gone by then. I just want to get some of those day-olds. The thought of a doughnut only made yesterday is about like heaven.

Two curly-haired kids, a little girl and an older boy, head down the street in my direction. I watch them approach. The dog stands alert and wags his tail. When they reach me, the girl holds out her arms and squeals, "A cute puppy!" She's about six or seven.

The boy, her brother I assume, could be about nine. He stands back with his hand on his sister's shoulder, protective-like.

The dog does a full-blown wiggle, and the girl squeals again. "Can I pet him?"

"Sure." I shrug.

She leans over and puts her arms around the dog's neck in a hug. At first I am worried that the dog might bite her—after all, I don't know what he's like. But he keeps wagging his tail, so I relax. I don't think I've ever seen such a friendly dog.

The boy steps closer. I can tell he wants to pet the dog, too, but he is hesitant. Maybe someone told him never to touch strange dogs.

"It's okay," I say. "You can pet him."

The boy eyes me suspiciously, but he taps the dog gently on the head. "He's a good dog," he says. "We had a dog that ran in the street and got hit."

The girl nods when he says this, and adds, "He died."

"Our mom won't let us get another one," the boy says.

The girl is scratching the dog under the chin now. He reaches his neck high and closes his eyes. His mouth turns up.

"Look! He's smiling!" the girl says. "He must like me!" She is grinning away at the same time, exposing a gap where her front baby teeth used to be. "What's his name?"

For some reason I can't tell them that the dog doesn't have a name—they think he belongs to me. So I make something up on the spot. "Shadow," I say, thinking how he's been following me all this time. "His name is Shadow."

The dog swishes proudly when I say it, and licks my hand.

"He knows his name!" the girl screams. "Shadow, Shadow, Shadow. Good dog, Shadow." Shadow rolls on his back in the grass with his long legs kicking in the air, and this makes all three of us laugh.

"Where's his collar? Where's his leash?" the boy asks.

"He doesn't need one," I answer.

"Shadow doesn't run away?" the boy asks.

"I guess not," I say.

"I want a dog like Shadow." The girl looks to her brother longingly. "I want a dog that don't run away."

"*Doesn't* run," he corrects. "Maybe someday. You have to prove that you won't leave the door open."

"I didn't *mean* to!" The girl's mood shifts suddenly, and she is about to cry. "It was an *accident!*"

The boy touches her on the shoulder. "It wasn't your fault," he says. "You didn't know any better. You're still little."

The girl is bawling now. "I am *not* little. I didn't *mean* to."

The boy looks at me for help. I shrug. "Come on," he says to his sister. "Let's go get our doughnuts. That will make you feel better."

This distracts the girl and she wipes her face. She pulls a bill from her pocket. "Look." She waves it in front of me. "I have five dollars."

"That's a lot of money," I say. I mean it, too. There was a time when five dollars was like a nickel to me, but now I think of what I could get with five dollars. Certainly a doughnut and coffee, and probably some fresh water, too. Even juice, or some bandages for my blisters.

The girl nods. "Tooth fairy gave it to me." She points to the gap in her mouth. "I'm getting as many doughnuts as I can. And, I'm going to eat them *all* myself." She grins at her brother.

He tugs her sleeve. "Let's go. Mommy will be mad if we don't get back soon."

The girl gives the dog a last hug. "Bye, Shadow," she says.

I watch them cross the street and go into the bakery. I put my hand on the dog's head. "Shadow," I say. His tail wags in all directions. His ears flatten and he nods.

About five minutes later the girl comes out with a pastry box. She's alone. She runs across the street, waddling in a little-girl way. She opens the box and takes out two doughnuts.

"Here," she says. "For you and Shadow." She hands me the doughnuts. "Don't tell my brother. He'd be mad."

She runs back across the street just as her brother comes out. They walk away. The girl looks behind her and waves. I wave back.

I eat one doughnut and most of the second. Shadow looks up at me expectantly. His eyes flicker with light. We stare at each other.

"Oh, all right." I hold out the last bit of doughnut, and he takes it ever so gingerly from my hand, then swallows it in one gulp. "I don't know how I'm going to feed you," I tell him. "I can't even feed myself. And I don't know where I'm going."

He looks at me like he doesn't care about any of that. He only cares about me.

"Suit yourself. It's a free country." I get up and we start walking. Shadow walks right next to me. I think to myself in the third person: *A girl named Blue and her dog, Shadow, walk on to face the unknown.*

I am developing blisters on top of my blisters, but still I walk. I've long since abandoned my disgust over eating old food. It's amazing what people will throw away.

I found an entire wrapped turkey sandwich in the dumpster behind a convenience store. Actually, Shadow led me to it. It was like finding gold. I ate the whole thing and haven't gotten sick yet. After days of eating hardly anything, it now seems there is plenty of food, especially if I'm willing to eat leftovers. Or perhaps I'm just less picky. As far as I know, Shadow survives this way all the time. He has a brilliant nose. He'll eat right off the ground.

I figure as long as I keep moving I'll be fine. No one pays attention to a girl who passes by once. If they see her twice, they might perk up. If they see her three times, they will remember and wonder. They might start asking questions and getting concerned. I can't let anyone see me more than once.

Sometimes I talk to Shadow, but mostly we are silent. I get the feeling that Shadow is deep in his own thoughts. Yet at the same time he is constantly watching, smelling, and listening. His ears rotate, picking up every sound.

By the late afternoon I come to a town with a large grassy park where there are enough people that I can blend in. There are nannies pushing baby carriages, toddlers screaming on the swings, picnickers picnicking, dogs being walked.

Shadow runs ahead to a chubby Lab, and they exchange a good sniff. The owner, a well-dressed woman, pulls the dog hard on its leash, even though both dogs are wagging tails, ready to play.

"Put that filthy mutt on a leash. There's a *law*, you know," she yells.

"Sorry," I mutter.

When Shadow comes bounding back I reprimand him. "Don't go getting us noticed. Or I will have to leash you, or worse, pretend we're not together." Shadow hangs his head in apology. "I know you just want to play." I hold on to his neck until the woman and her dog are gone.

I get to the public restrooms; this one has a working water fountain outside. "I think it may be time for a bath," I tell Shadow.

He runs away from me as if he knows what I am about to do. I chase after him. "Come on," I call. "It's only a little water." He stops, waits until I get close, and then runs again. He does this several times, but he is grinning like it's a game.

Finally I catch up to him, and begrudgingly he lets me steer him back to the fountain. "It'll feel good," I say. "You'll see." I fill my water bottle and pour the water over him several times to make sure he's wet through all his layers of fur.

I feel bad, but I can't help laughing. He looks pathetic. "You're such a brave dog, how can you be scared of a little water?"

After he is thoroughly wet I start massaging him, and he totally loves that. "See? It's not so bad," I say. "Wait here," I instruct. "I have an idea."

I go into the bathroom and fill my hands with frothy pink soap from the dispenser. I take it back out and rub it all over Shadow, then rinse him once more. He does an extra big shake, splattering me all over, but I don't care.

Turns out he's not gray after all, but much lighter, more of a soft silver, with streaks of white down his back and on his tail.

He grins, as if to say *I told you so*. Then he runs circles in the grass, rolling around to dry off.

"You're not a filthy mutt now. You look like a prize pedigree and a handsome one at that," I say. I find a good-size stick and we play fetch. He gallops after it and prances back to me.

For a few minutes I imagine I am just a girl playing with her dog in the park. Maybe I live nearby where a doting mom waits for me. I'll come home from my walk and she'll greet me at the door with a plate of hot chocolate chip cookies, a glass of milk, and a biscuit for Shadow.

Shadow trots to a garbage pail and barks. So much for chocolate chip cookies. I peer inside, trying to be casual. A quick glance can tell me a lot. What kind of trash is on top hints at what may be underneath. This one has the typical coffee cups, plastic bags, and chip wrappers. I sift around and find one lone sandal under a chip bag. The strap is broken, but if there's a shoe, what else could there be?

I search deeper. I find a ripped notebook, an empty pencil case, and a faded orange backpack.

I hold the pack to Shadow's nose. "How's it smell?" I ask. He sniffs it and nods. I move my head closer and take a whiff. "Not bad." I turn the bag around and check its compartments and zippers. The mesh side is ripped, and a zipper on one of the outer pockets is stuck, but otherwise it's fine.

I take the mini-flashlight from my pocket. The key still dangles from its chain. I finger the metal grooves. I don't know why I even have it. I take it off the chain and fling it into the garbage can. As it clinks against the side it echoes: *Gone. Gone. Gone.* It disappears under the trash and the echo stops. I panic. What have I done? I reach in to find it, but Shadow nudges my hand and stops me. "You're right," I say. "It's a useless key."

I put the flashlight in one of the side pockets of the pack. "Okay?" I ask. Shadow nods.

. . .

Finding the pack in the garbage has given me an idea. On the edge of the town I come to a sidewalk mall. It's late enough so that everything is closed, but at the end of the parking lot I find what I am looking for—a dark blue Salvation Army bin filled with people's throwaways.

"You keep guard," I tell Shadow. It's a narrow opening, but I hoist myself up and crawl inside. It smells of a mixture of mildew, cigarettes, bubblegum, and cat pee. There is only a sliver of moonlight shining in. I use the flashlight to get a better look.

Once I get used to the smell it's like Christmas, going through it all. At first I grab everything I can—shirts, sweaters, a really pretty flowery dress. As my pile grows I realize my stupidity. I don't need things like dresses now, even if they are pretty. Whatever I take I have to carry. I carefully select only the practical: a pair of jeans, sweatpants, two long-sleeved shirts, one fleece jacket.

I look for shoes. The Converse sneakers have no arch support, not to mention the blisters. Something like hiking boots would be great, but even just a pair of regular sneakers would be better. All I find are useless heels and pumps or men's shoes that are way too large.

I take off my shorts and filthy shirt and put on the jeans and one of the shirts. It's like wearing brand-new clothes. I pack the rest in tight rolls. I am about to hop out, but before I do, Shadow hops in. He sniffs, then circles around on a pile and curls up into a small ball.

"What are you doing?" I ask.

He lifts his head and yawns.

I lie down next to Shadow.

He snuggles against me, and I give in to the first soft, satisfying sleep I can remember.


At the first crack of morning light, I pack my new items and Shadow and I hop out. We find bread and some brown bananas in a dumpster for breakfast. Then we head toward the rising sun, staying on the country roads.

The next place I come to is a café called the Bean. It's much cleaner and more inviting than some of the other places I've stopped at. Looks more like a college hangout. I could be near a university. I give Shadow a pat and tell him to wait. He sniffs around the outdoor tables searching for crumbs. I take a deep breath and go inside.

I head toward the bathroom in the back, avoiding any eye contact with the few customers. Thankfully it doesn't require a key, so I don't have to go up and ask anyone. I wash my hands and face, wet down my hair. I wish I had some shampoo—I hate the feeling of greasy hair.

Once when my dad was on a nature kick he took us camping. I must have been about ten. The whole experience was gross—the tent, the sleeping bags, the mosquitoes. But the worst part was being dirty. I couldn't stand even one day with dirty hair, so I washed it in the camp spigot. I stuck my head under the faucet and used a cup to get the back part wet. I didn't have any shampoo, so I just used soap, which I couldn't completely rinse out. My hair stayed flat and funny-looking all day. But that's tame compared to what I look like now.

Why can I remember such a mundane thing like washing my hair at a campsite seven years ago, yet I can't remember anything that happened seven days ago?

I concentrate. I remember things about my mother and father. I remember when both of them read to me at bedtime. They read a book called *Frog and Toad*, acting out the characters together in different voices. We all laughed hysterically.

But then gradually, over the years, without my even noticing, they stopped. In fact, I stopped wanting to do anything with them. I wanted to be alone more and more. I wanted to cry all the time. My parents said they didn't know what to do with me, they just wanted me to be happy. Was I ever happy?

I remember school. I was smart, but not enough to really do anything special or to get into a good college. I knew people and I didn't have any enemies, but I didn't have any real friends, either. I didn't like school.

I remember my house and especially my room. I liked my old Victorian house. I was happy in my room with the mural of trees.

And then, of course, I remember Jake. I liked Jake. Jake liked me. He had made me happy, hadn't he? We were a couple, weren't we? We did things, didn't we?

But that's when it stops and I can't remember anything else. When was all that? And where are they all now?

I've hardly heard the awful chant for a while, not since Shadow started walking with me, but it starts to come back now. Slow and quiet at first, then louder: *All dead. All dead. No one survived.*

I want to throw up. I splash my face with cold water and rub my temples. I count my breaths. I stop trying to remember. I am here and this is now, and that's all that matters. The chant goes away.

When I exit the bathroom I scan the café. The place is cozy, with comfy chairs and a velvet burgundy couch by the window. I could take a nap on that couch—sink myself right into the plushness, disappear between the cushions and sleep forever. It looks so soft, so easy and mindless. But I don't risk the couch—too close to the window and too obvious. I can't take any chances.

There's free filtered water on the counter with the milks and sugars. I pour myself a cup. I drink it in one gulp, drink a second, and take a third, along with a handful of sugar packets, and go sit in one of the armchairs in the back. The chair wraps around me.

I sit back and watch, quiet and invisible as a mouse. A pregnant mother and her toddler boy are to my right. The boy smears his face with cream cheese and laughs. The mother tries to wipe it off, and he just laughs harder, then hiccups. This sends him into a giggle fit, and he starts snorting. The mother starts laughing, too, and holds her big belly. They are so happy they make me smile.

The toddler suddenly jumps up and runs past me. His mother follows in hot pursuit and catches him before he gets out the door. She gathers their things and they go out together.

I notice that they left almost an entire half of the bagel on the table. I glide over to their table and pretend it's my seat. I make sure no one sees me and bite into the leftover bagel. Delicious.

As I'm finishing, two soccer moms with fancy coffees and

biscotti sit at the table next to me. They start a very loud conversation.

Mom 1: You're so thin these days. How do you do it?

Mom 2: I joined the Loser Club and lost thirteen pounds. It might be time to buy a new bathing suit, even though swimming season is over.

Mom 1: I can't even try on suits. Not until I reach my goal. I lose and gain like a yo-yo. Do they make you exercise a lot?

Mom 2: Mainly walking. They say walking twenty minutes a day is enough to keep the average person healthy.

Mom 1: I probably get that just from going up and down the stairs checking on that idiot contractor.

Mom 2: How's the remodeling going?

Mom 1: It's a headache. Dan wants us to switch over to natural gas instead of oil.

Mom 2: Didn't you hear about that house?

Mom 1: What house?

Mom 2: There was a house in some new development that blew up. Everybody died.

These words catch me off-guard. The bagel and cream cheese sting the back of my throat. I stand up too fast and get a head rush and have to sit back down. *Everybody died.*

The women stop talking and notice me. "Are you all right, dear?" one of them asks.

I need air. I have to get out. I stand again, slowly this time. The two women are staring at me. I nod blankly, and they seem to accept that and go back to their conversation like nothing happened. "Really, you should try the Loser Club. It could change your life."

I manage to get out before I double over from the pain in my stomach. *All dead, all dead* is loud and strong. Panicked voices are screaming inside my head. Everything is hazy. I crouch on the sidewalk and hold my hands over my ears.

Through all the noise I hear a small voice laughing. It's a real voice. The pregnant woman and her toddler are walking down the sidewalk toward me. The toddler points. "Doggie, doggie!" Shadow is right next to me. I hadn't even noticed. I put my hand on his back and breathe.

"Yes, look at the nice doggie," the mother says.

The toddler reaches his fingers toward Shadow. Shadow wiggles over and gives them a lick.

"Nice doggie," the mother says again. She puts her hand on my shoulder. "Are you all right?" she asks.

I muster all of my energy to stand. "I'm okay," I whisper. I start to walk down the street, one foot in front of the other. Like nothing happened.

I know the woman is watching me and I hear the boy's sweet giggle, but I don't look back.

# Before

I ran all the way to Jake's house for our very first date. I was puffed out by the time I got to his door. I rearranged my stretchy black dress and rang the bell.

"Hey," he said.

"Hey," I said, catching my breath and wiping some sweat from my forehead. Great. He was going to think I was always sweaty.

But he didn't mention it. Instead he said, "You look nice."

The way he was looking at my chest I could tell the cleavage worked, though it suddenly made me a little uncomfortable.

I smiled. "You, too." He was wearing black jeans and a spanking white T-shirt. He smelled of after-shave.

We got into his car. It was some kind of fancy sports car, bright red and super shiny.

"I just got a new sound system," he said. He leaned across to turn up the volume, and as he did his arm brushed against mine. Did he touch me on purpose?

"Listen to these babies." He closed his eyes and bobbed his head to the beat.

We drove for ten minutes without saying anything. He couldn't have heard me over the music anyway, but I was grateful, since I wasn't sure what to say. I'd never been alone in a car with a boy before.

Jake's dad's gallery was in town, but we headed in the opposite direction, toward the bay. Jake drove up the big hill and then finally stopped at the park overlooking the water and the islands. He stopped the car but kept the music on.

"What about the opening?" I shouted.

Jake turned the volume down. "Let's bag it. No one will notice if we're not there." He wrapped his hand around my arm. "We can find better things to do," he said.

He reached into the glove compartment and took out a joint and a lighter. "You smoke?" he asked as he lit the joint and offered it to me.

"No," I said. I knew pot wasn't as terrible as parents and teachers made out. I knew people who had tried it before, but still, I didn't want to risk losing control in the midst of my first date. Who knew what a fool I could make of myself?

"You sure?" he asked.

"Yeah. I mean, no thanks."

"I was sure you'd be into weed. But that's okay. I like a girl who's a bit of a straight priss. Kind of sexy. You don't mind if I have some, do you?"

I shook my head. Did he just call me a priss and say I was sexy at the same time? I wasn't sure if I should be offended or flattered. I decided to be flattered. No one had ever called me sexy.

He took a drag, coughed, took another, then put it out and placed it in the cup holder. I wanted that moment from the day before to come back—when we convened with nature together, when there was electricity.

I slowly reached my arm out and touched his cheek. He leaned over, bringing his face close to mine. "Where have you been hiding all this time?" he whispered. "I mean, I know you've lived nearby and all, but how come I never really noticed you before?"

I was going to say that he had noticed me once, even gave me flowers and asked me to marry him, but if he didn't remember that incident, I didn't exactly want to remind him.

He grabbed my shoulders and turned me so we were facing. It was awkward and uncomfortable, but I could tell we were going to kiss. His mouth swallowed me whole and I no longer felt anything else. It was a kiss full of tenderness, like he knew what he was doing. A guy like Jake had probably kissed a lot of girls. I ran my hands through his hair like I'd seen in movies, and he moved his down to my thighs. Was this real?

I'd never thought in a million years that this would happen to me, that someone could like me enough to touch me this way, that it could be someone like Jake, and that it could happen so suddenly with no warning. Why was Jake suddenly into me? Then I felt his tongue and I didn't care if it was real or why it was happening. I just let my body respond, and the electricity came back.

Just as I was thinking I could kiss like this forever, a car drove up. Its headlights beamed straight through the window, and we broke apart instantly. A door opened and a voice bellowed, "Police! Come out with your hands up!"

Jake swore and shoved the remaining joint back into the glove compartment.

What on earth would my parents do if they found out I'd been alone in a car with a boy *and* smoking pot? Even if I hadn't smoked any, they would assume I had. "Can we go to jail?" I asked.

Jake looked like he was about to laugh, then stopped himself.

A head peered in the window. "Any left for me?" It was not a cop, but a guy named Bradley. I recognized him from school. He had been one of Jake's friends who laughed at me during the swim-noodle incident. He was still in Jake's popular group. At least he had been when Jake left. Jake had changed since then. Bradley had not.

"Idiot," Jake said. "You about scared us half to death."

Bradley poked his head in farther. He did a double take when he saw me, probably wondering what I was doing there with Jake. He nodded and said, "Hey," then punched Jake in the shoulder. "Dude, you're really going for it, aren't you?"

"Shut up," Jake said. They whispered something so low I couldn't hear.

Bradley stood back. "I was just leaving anyway. Obviously three's a crowd. Adrianna is looking for you. Said she had something important to tell you."

"What could she possibly have left to say? I told her it was over." Jake turned to me. "Don't listen to this dumb-wad."

"Whatever," Bradley said. "I'm outta here." He got back into his car, beeped twice, then drove away. Jake moved toward me again, but it didn't feel right anymore. It was all too fast.

"I should get home," I said. The magic was over.

# Now

Morning becomes noon. Noon becomes afternoon. Afternoon becomes dusk. Then comes the night. At least at night no one can see me, but the dark brings its own share of worry and fear. I don't know what may be in the shadows.

I walk by some sort of utility company with large, round containers that glow like fallen moons. It's all sectioned off with barbed wire and DANGER NO TRESPASSING signs. It's hard to tell if it's still in business. The fence is rusty and the grounds around it are grown up with weeds.

I say to Shadow, "I'm tired. I have to stop."

He keeps plodding ahead, though, and I follow in spite of my complaining body. We reach an underpass of a highway bridge. At the top of the incline over some low bushes and a hill of rubble is a flickering of light and voices. I stop, fearful of the people, but Shadow keeps going, so I take that as a good sign.

It's hard to tell for sure with their baggy clothes and ragged faces, but I think there are two men and one woman. They are huddled in a circle around a metal garbage can. The light is from a fire inside the can. Embers crackle and rise into the air, making their faces glow. The sound, the smell, the image, all make me uncomfortable. I don't like fire.

The woman turns to me. "Getting chilly already, isn't it?" She beckons me closer. "Come share the warmth. It's okay. We won't bite."

The two men smile as if to confirm.

There are empty liquor bottles and bits of trash around, as well as some sleeping bags and mats set up along the ridge under the bridge on a small stretch of dirt. A fourth person is crouched on the ground away from the others. His hands are clasped around his knees, and he's rocking back and forth, muttering one swear-word after another.

The sound of a car driving over the bridge above echoes for a minute, then all is quiet again except for the occasional crackle of the fire and the crouching man's mumbling. The others don't pay him any mind.

The woman hands me a bottle of amber-colored liquid. "Here," she says. "Have some whiskey."

I take a swig. It's warm and soothing going down, and then slowly it starts to burn. I cough and hand it back.

The crouching man lifts his head, suddenly noticing me. He stares intensely. He has long hair and a long beard, a fiery face, and a bulbous nose. He looks like a skinny Santa, without the jolly laugh. His eyes pierce right through me, and I get a prickly feeling. Shadow starts to growl and the man scowls and moves away.

"Don't mind Jimbo," the woman says. "He had a rough day. He needs to sleep it off. You from around here?"

I shake my head.

"Traveling, then?"

I nod.

"Well, you got to sleep. It's late and night is no good for traveling alone. Even with a dog. There's an extra mat if you like."

One of the men, the shorter of the two, hands me a can of beans. They've been sharing it, all using the same fork. I know it'd be crazy for me to ask if they have a clean one, so I take a forkful and shove it into my mouth. The beans are dry and bland, so when the whiskey bottle comes back to me I take another swig to wash them down.

They start talking about Jimbo. "Got his ass kicked by some rich kids having their way," the guy who gave me the beans says.

Then the second guy: "Jimbo don't like to have his ego wounded."

First guy: "He told me he pulled his knife and cut one of them. That got them running."

Second guy: "Serves them right. They were picking on him for no reason, other than he's old and homeless."

"Still, violence isn't the way." This from the woman.

"What is the way, then? Get beat to death?" the first guy says.

I tune them out. My head is spinning, maybe from the drink or maybe from exhaustion. "Can I lie down?" I ask, even though they'd already offered.

The woman points to one of the mats. She takes off her trench coat and hands it to me. "Use this for a blanket."

It's dirty and smelly, but I don't refuse.

I look around for the creepy guy, the one they call Jimbo, but he's not there anymore. I walk a few steps to the ridge and lie down on one of the mats. I pull the coat over me. Shadow snuggles with me, and I hold on to him for protection.

The next thing I know Shadow is sitting up and growling low. It's still dark but a trace of dawn is in the air. The fire has gone out. At first I don't see anything, then my eyes focus on a man standing above me. He looks ghostly. The prickly feeling comes back, this time like extra-sharp pins in my neck. It's Jimbo.

"What . . ." I stumble as I stand, clutching my backpack close. "What do you want?"

He grins. His gums are covered in black spots, and he has a couple of missing teeth. The other three from last night are nowhere around. It is just him and me. And Shadow.

Shadow curls his lips to reveal his sharp incisors and lets out a long, low growl from deep inside. His hackles rise and he seems to grow to twice his size. He is suddenly large and looming. More wolf than dog. He looks so different, so scary.

The man steps back. "Control that dog," he warns, drawing out the words slowly.

"Sorry," I mumble. I try to grab hold of Shadow's neck to steer him away, but he shakes me off. He won't let me touch him. His growl turns into fierce barking.

"I'll kill it if it comes near me." The man lifts his shirt to reveal a thick knife handle tucked into the waist of his pants. He stares straight at me. "You and I are just the same, you know. Don't go thinking you're any different."

The man pulls out his knife and waves it in the air.

I go numb. I am going to die. I have a sudden realization that death might be better than life, if I could only just accept it. I won't be the only one dead. Others have died. But how? Where? Why?

Shadow stops barking and stands still. He stares at the man. The man stares back. It is incredibly quiet, as if everything has suddenly frozen. Even the air has stopped. My eyes dart from Shadow to the man. They are in some kind of trance. It's eerie, like nothing else exists. The only things moving are Shadow's eyes, swirling like a mad fire.

It lasts only a second, maybe two. Shadow shakes and things start moving again. The man backs away. "We're the same," he hisses. Shadow growls again and the man turns and runs. As he does he lets go of his knife. It falls to the ground with a clunk, but he doesn't stop. He keeps running into the mist until he's out in the road and disappears around a bend.

The sun creeps its light under the bridge. Somewhere a bird calls and another answers. The man is gone and Shadow is normal again.

I pick up the knife. I wrap the blade in one of my extra shirts and place it carefully in my pack.

Another day of endless walking, and by nightfall not only do my legs ache, they itch like crazy. My broken blisters rub raw against the canvas of my sneakers. I wince in pain with each step. Forget trying to be the steadfast ant. I am in pain, and there are no cows in the fields to encourage me. Shadow tries—he runs ahead, runs back, circles me, licks my hand, but I merely drag myself along.

I stop at an all-night convenience store and grab handfuls of paper towel from the bathroom. I sit behind the store and peel off my shoes. As I suspected, the blisters are raw and oozing. First I carefully cut off the flapping skin, using the tip of Jimbo's knife. Then I wrap the paper towels around my heels and stuff my feet back into the sneakers. The sneakers feel a little tight now, but it's a lot better than the chafing.

It is a clear night with a sliver of moon and stars. I chow down on a dumpster dinner of chicken wings and some kind of Chinese egg rolls. I give some of both to Shadow. I climb over the railing and walk into the woods, using the flashlight. Its glow is weak; I don't know how much longer the battery will last. Shadow leads, so I turn off the light and follow him. The white parts of his fur reflect the moon. He is a ghost dog in the night.

All of a sudden I snag a root and lose balance. I feel myself falling. I think maybe I can stop the fall and regain balance, but it's too late. I lose touch with gravity, and down I go. A sharp branch scrapes along my cheek, and *thunk*. I am face-down in a pile of leaves.

I lie there, smelling the damp earth. My body throbs along with my heart. I guess this means I am still alive, though I kind of wish I wasn't. My cheek stings. I feel like an idiot even though no one is there to see me.

This is my life—walking, fleeing, hiding, aching, going nowhere, having nothing.

Then Shadow's warm, wet tongue licks me and the sting lessens. Slowly I sit up. I touch my cheek where there is already a welt forming. I wave the swarms of mosquitoes from around my head, but they don't stay away for long. They are too keen to suck my blood.

My knee is scraped. I wipe it off and wipe my eyes with my dirty sleeve. I stand. "I'm okay," I tell Shadow.

We walk until we come to a moss-covered opening surrounded by a couple of boulders. I clear away some dead branches and lie down. The moss makes a nice soft padding. Shadow cuddles next to me. At first everything is quiet, and then sounds slowly emerge. The bellow of a bullfrog, the hoot of an owl, the gabble of migrating geese. For a moment I forget my pain, my fears, my uncertainty, and in a strange way, everything is peaceful.

I watch the stars twinkling through the trees. I've never seen so many stars. I know the names of constellations like the Big Dipper, Orion's Belt, Cassiopeia, but I've never actually seen them. I try to make out something that looks like a big dipping spoon or the belt of a man, but there's no way I can identify anything like that. I realize I don't even know what Cassiopeia is supposed to be.

I always thought all stars were the same, but each one has its own identity. Some are bigger than others, some blink, and some shine steady; some are reddish, while others are white. Some are planets, I know, but I don't know which ones. There is a whole world up there.

I start to think that maybe we are not all alone in this solar system. How would someone like me look from up there? I'd be a teeny-tiny little ant, or I'd be nothing at all, not even visible.

I am almost asleep when Shadow jumps up suddenly. He whimpers, staring straight ahead. I follow his gaze through the trees. I don't see anything, but Shadow's ears are alert. He is listening and staring intently. He whimpers again and growls low. I grab the light and shine it in his direction. It produces a dim beam and then fades to nothing.

"What?" I whisper. "What is it?"

Shadow circles me with his tail between his legs. My heart races and my mind fills with thoughts of danger. If Shadow is scared, then I ought to be doubly scared. After all, I am a girl alone in the woods in the middle of night.

Slowly I creep my arm over to grab my pack and find the knife. I clutch it to my chest. I hear the crunching sound of feet on leaves. Is it animal or human? I am too afraid to sit up, so I just lie there, tightening my grip on the knife handle.

I watch Shadow watching whatever it is. We wait forever for something to emerge.

Then there is a movement in the bushes and the leaves shake. I close my eyes and scream, preparing for the worst. When nothing happens I open my eyes. My mouth is still open, but no sound comes out.

A little animal pokes through. It could be a possum, a fat rat. I'm not sure. It doesn't have the black and white markings of a skunk, and it's not a raccoon. It's gray with a long, skinny furless tail. It looks just as startled to see me as I am to see it. I'm so relieved, I start to laugh. It stops for a second, figures I am not an enemy. Shadow does nothing more than sniff it as it waddles on by.

We wait until it's completely gone. The owl hoots. The night goes back to before. I release my grip on the knife. Shadow relaxes his ears. He circles three times in the same place, then lies down tucked against my shoulder. He lets out a big sigh and closes his eyes.

"You're a good dog," I say. I pat him on the rump and hold him close all night long.

# BEFORE

Everyone wants to know about sex. As soon as you start dating someone, that's all they care about. "Did you do it?" "Is he a good kisser?" "How was it?" "Where was it?" "Did you use protection?"

The thing with Jake—it was more than that. It couldn't be condensed to a few stupid logistical questions about one act, not that anyone knew Jake and I were going out. I wasn't even sure if we were. I couldn't believe that Jake actually liked me. I was in some kind of dream.

We had gone on three dates, if you could call them that, mostly parking and making out, places where we were almost always alone. He said it was because he wanted me all to himself, which was fine with me because I doubted his popular friends would like me. Once he took me to a fancy sushi restaurant where I ordered chicken tenders while I watched him eat slimy, raw pieces of fish and tried not to gag.

Our fourth date was Sunday afternoon (our first daytime

date), and we were going to the beach. Which meant he'd have to see me in a bathing suit.

I owned three suits. My regular solid tank was ugly and stretched out already. The string bikini I'd bought but never worn was obviously out of the question. So I settled on a blue tankini. Blue was my favorite color and I figured I'd have the option of showing a little skin if I got bold enough. I wore a loose T-shirt and shorts over it.

I assumed we would go to one of the pristine beaches out of town, but when I got into the car, Jake said, "Let's go to the town beach. You're down with that, right?"

I didn't mind the town beach at all. In fact, I kind of liked it. There were always empty beer cans and random litter strewn about, but there was something "real" about it. In the summer kids splashed in and out of the freezing water; in the winter couples huddled together smoking cigarettes. You could do what you wanted there and no one cared. I was surprised that Jake would like it, though. He wasn't a town-beach kind of guy. He was more a yacht-in-the-Caribbean kind of guy.

It was late in the afternoon, so all the little kids were gone by the time we got there. A few couples walked along the shore. A group of older teens, college kids by the looks of it, had a boom box, so loud rock music filled the air. I watched a circle of gulls follow a boat out in the bay. A dog barked after them while its owner trailed behind.

"Is this an okay spot?" Jake asked.

"Can we move away from that dog?" I asked. "I don't want it to walk on our stuff."

We found a spot and laid out our towels. I took off my shorts and top. I was painfully aware of Jake watching me. He smiled and peeled himself out of his shirt. He had a clean, smooth chest, and you could see his abs. He definitely worked out. I pulled on my tankini top to cover my belly and crossed my arms over my chest. I wasn't bold enough to show that much skin yet.

"Last one in is a loser." He ran down toward the water.

"Not fair!" I called, running after him. "You didn't give me warning."

Jake reached the water and waited for me to catch up. "Okay. Let's go together, then."

He counted to three and we dove under only to rise up screaming from the icy shock. Jake grabbed me by the shoulders and dunked me. I swam a few laps around him. I've always liked being in the water. It's the one place where I can forget about my body and everything else. It's like nothing matters under water. I was smiling when I came back up. Jake leaned over and we kissed. I felt like a new person. Relaxed and happy. This was the magic I wanted.

After about ten minutes of dunking, splashing, and kissing, we ran to our towels to warm up. I lay on my front and stared out at the ocean. The sea and the sky were almost the same color.

"It's all blue," I mused. "Nothing but blue as far as you can see. But if you put air or water in a glass, it's clear. Why is that?"

Jake shrugged. "Something to do with reflection of light, I think," he said.

"It's so beautiful."

"Yeah, but it's all an illusion." Jake picked up a tube of sunscreen. "Let me put this on your back. You don't want to get burned." He straddled me and moved my hair out of the way. He started massaging my shoulders with lotion.

"You have gorgeous hair," he said. "Especially when it's wet and sleeked back. Really sexy."

He rolled over next to me. He put his hand on my thigh, then moved it slowly to my hip, then waist, and kept slipping it up. Then he moved back down again, then up, then down, caressing my body. He tucked some strands of my hair behind my ear and whispered, "Let's get out of here."

We went back to the car. We kissed more passionately than ever before.

"Do you want to?" he asked.

"Yes," I said. I did. I did want to. I wanted Jake to love me. He scrambled into the back seat and I followed, banging my head on the roof as I climbed over the seat.

He fumbled out of his suit. I took off my bottoms but left the top part on.

"Wait a sec." Jake leaned over and took something out of his wallet. A condom. He put it on like he was a pro.

For some reason this struck me as funny. I was going to have sex with the cool guy in a car at the beach. I burst out in laughter.

"What's wrong?" he asked.

"Nothing," I said. "It's just . . . I don't know . . . this seems funny."

"I thought you wanted to."

"No, I mean, yes. I do, but it's just that I didn't believe this would ever happen."

"It's happening," he said.

He lifted my hips and I sat on his lap. "Mmm. Can you take your top off?"

"I don't know," I said. He could see my stomach and all, but I wasn't sure I was ready for him to see everything. He didn't ask again, and I respected him for that. He held my neck and then moved his hands to my back, gripping tightly.

I watched out the rear window at the sun shimmering like crystal on the tips of the small waves. The same little dog from earlier was splashing in and out of the water. The owner was smiling and laughing like she was having the time of her life just watching her dog play.

I was surprised when Jake let out a deep breath and moved me off his lap.

"Man oh man," he said. "It just happened so fast. I couldn't wait."

"Oh." I didn't know what to say. I had felt something, but I wasn't sure if it was what I was supposed to feel. He was acting like it was all over and I still wanted to keep kissing and touching. I wrapped my arms around his back. I wanted him close. I wanted to be with him forever. I wanted him to love me and me to love him. I wanted to be important.

"Do I matter?" I asked.

He unwrapped my arms and worked his way back into his shorts and T-shirt. "What kind of question is that?"

"I don't know." I found my bathing suit bottoms and put them on. Then I asked again, "Do I matter? Am I important?"

He turned my hand over and put his lips on my palm. "I wouldn't have done this if I didn't think you were just fine." He pinched my butt. "I like that you have a little extra to squeeze." He took something out of his pocket. It was a thin, colorful braided rope. "This is for you."

"What is it?" I asked.

"It's a friendship bracelet. Don't you know about friendship bracelets? All the girls wear them. But this one is special. This means we are more than friends." He tied the bracelet in a double knot around my wrist. "So you'll remember me."

As if I could ever forget.

# Now

I don't know when I fell asleep, but at some point night sounds stopped and morning sounds began.

The dawn sky is a grayish purple at first, and then turns pink. The sun rises through the trees, and slowly everything brightens. I always thought a sunrise looked the same as a sunset, but it's not the same at all. Dawn is soft and quiet, as though it wants to wake the world up gently. Whereas sunsets are so bright and electric they almost seem to scream, *Hey! Day is done! Go to bed!* It seems it should be the opposite.

Shadow is still nuzzled under my shoulder. He fits there in a tight ball. His back legs are curled under him, and his chin rests on his front paws. It's amazing how small he can make himself. His cheeks flutter a little bit as he breathes. Every once in a while he makes a small whinny, like a tiny horse. His eyes flicker back and forth under his lids. Perhaps he is dreaming of chasing squir-rels or rolling in the grass, or maybe he's dreaming of a comfortable, plush dog bed—the fancy, expensive designer kind. Stuff he'll never get from me.

I stroke his nose. He murmurs a little. He lets out a deep sigh from way down, then yawns awake. Our eyes lock and I swear we are telecommunicating. The gold flecks in his eyes glimmer.

"I need you," I say out loud.

He curls back his mouth and smiles. And then it's like he actually is talking and I can hear him.

*I need you, too,* he says.

He breaks the gaze and does a perfect downward dog stretch and then shakes from head to tail, like nothing happened. It must have been my imagination.

My stomach releases its now familiar grumble. I don't think I have ever been truly hungry in my life, up until now. There were girls at school who bragged about how many days they could go without eating, how they craved emptiness more than food, but I was never one of them. I've always liked eating, even if my parents said I was fussier than a baby about what I ate.

Though fussiness is not a problem anymore. Now I'm happy if I can find a crust of bread—I don't care if it's white or wheat or full of vegetables.

I take a drink of water, then pour some into a cup for Shadow. I try to work out the gnarls in my hair. I know I'm probably starting to smell worse. I can still feel the welt on my cheek where the branch swiped me. There are mosquito bites on top of mosquito bites, but they hardly itch anymore. I remember the frog from last night. That means there must be a pond nearby.

"Do you know if there's water around here?" I ask Shadow.

He leads me through the woods to a pond. I don't know if it could be called a pond exactly, but it is a body of water and it's big enough for me to submerge. There's algae around the edge, but the center is clean. A morning mist rises from the surface. I take off my shoes first and then the rest of my clothes, glancing around nervously. I've never been naked outside. I fold my clothes into a tidy pile.

A breeze whispers around my body as I kick aside the algae and dip my toes in. The muddy bottom is soft and squishy. I wade in farther and it gets colder.

It's only thigh-high, but I paddle around for a minute until I'm used to the cold, then duck my head under. I heard somewhere that in the old days people used to clean themselves with leaves and mud, so I take some from the brink and rub myself down, then dive under again.

When I'm done I dry off with my T-shirt and put on my second pair of clothes. I rinse and wring out the clothes I've been wearing and drape them over some branches to dry. This will make them smell like muddy pond water, but it will be a vast improvement from how they were smelling.

I sit by the pond and wait. I suddenly wish I had a book to read. I can't even recall the last book I read for fun, not since I was in grade school at least. I play with a stick, making shapes in the mud and letting them fill with water. Shadow splashes around in the pond chasing bugs.

"Why am I here?" I ask out loud. Shadow stops his game and comes over. He raises his eyes and looks into mine. "Do you know what is wrong?" I study his eyes. "I believe you do know, but you can't say, can you?" Shadow ignores me and wades into the water again.

A stream of light pokes through the trees and sparkles off the blade of Jimbo's knife on the ground with the rest of my stuff. It is not a long knife, about eight or nine inches, with a thick, black metal handle. I pick it up and turn it around in my hand.

*You have power.* A voice echoes as though it's someone other than me, telling me what to do. It is definitely coming from inside, but it's not the same as the chanting voice, and it is definitely not Shadow.

I hold the blade up to my face. A distorted, fuzzy image of me reflects back.

*You have the power to end your life. Here. Now. No one would know. No one would care. You would be free.* The voice is so clear, but it's all monotone. There's no feeling in it, which makes it eerily convincing.

Shadow is swimming across the pond. He can't see me. He wouldn't notice if this blade slipped into a vein in my neck. He wouldn't notice until the blood came gushing, and then he'd be too late to save me.

*He can't save you anyway. He's just a dog.*

I hold the knife inches from my face. I stare at my reflection in the blade, then shift my gaze to Shadow, then back to me, back to Shadow, me, Shadow, me, Shadow.

Shadow reaches the other side and turns around. His head bobs on the surface like a glowing buoy. I am still holding the knife in the same position when he slithers out of the water and shakes, sprinkling droplets all over me. Shadow stares at the knife, then at me.

*If you have the power to end your life, you have the power to live it, too.* It's not the strange voice anymore. It's coming from Shadow this time.

I look at him—his mouth doesn't move. He's not actually talking, but I hear his voice loud and clear. I don't know how I know, but I am certain it is him. It's like Shadow and I can understand each other all of a sudden. It's not my imagination. It can't be. He says again, *You have the power to live.*

He may be right. I could die any number of ways. I probably will, so why do it myself? There may come a better time, a time when I absolutely need to die, but is that time now? I put the knife down.

I sit there for a while thinking about appropriate ways, times, and places to die. I think about it casually, as though life and death are nothing more than day and night. I mindlessly try to comb out the knots in my hair with a stick. It's useless—the stick gets caught in all the tangles.

I pick up the knife once more, but this time it has a better purpose. I pull my hair into a ponytail and slice through. My hair is resistant, but eventually I hold my ponytail out in front of me.

My head feels instantly better. "There," I say. I lay the hair on the ground.

"What now?" I ask. I can see my reflection in Shadow's eyes. I rub my scalp and tousle my cropped hair with my fingers.

*You know,* he says. *You know.*

I fiddle with my bracelet. Shadow is right, I do know. I know I have to keep going until I get to the house where I belong. Back to my room. Back to the sea. Back to where I matter. Back home. That's where the answers are. That is my reason to keep going, my reason to live. When I get there everything will be clear again. I will have shelter. I will have love.

"Are you coming with me?" I ask.

*Of course, silly,* he says.

"You're not just a dog, are you?" I ask.

He nuzzles his nose under my hand, but he doesn't answer. He gets up and starts walking. I wrap the knife in one of the shirts and put it and the rest of my clothes into my pack.

When I get to the road I look in both directions, then head toward the rising pink sun. East toward the sea.

It's too early for traffic, and it's not a busy road to begin with. The temperature is mild with an autumn nip. Colors are starting to appear in the trees, and everything crackles and glows. Shadow walks ahead but keeps turning around to beckon me onward. *Come on. One step, then another and another. We'll get there.*

Hitchhiking is dangerous. Hitchhiking means crazy people will rape and murder you and cut your body into a million little pieces and bury them one by one or toss them into the sea. At least that is what happens to teenagers who hitchhike in the movies and on TV. So no one hitches anymore. Not like they used to—or like we assume they used to in the old days when there weren't as many rapists and murderers driving around and hitching wasn't the dangerous, deadly means of travel that it is supposed to be today.

I haven't yet stuck my thumb out, but I have renewed energy, so when I hear a car in the distance behind me I think now is the time to start. The car slows down when it nears me. It's an old small hatchback, a "safe" car. The window opens and a young woman smiles.

"Where you headed?" she asks. She has a soft, girlie voice. She doesn't seem much older than me.

"East," I say.

"It's awfully early to be hitching all the way out here." She sizes me up.

I hesitate. Even though I am talking to this stranger, I still have to be careful what I say.

"I'm not going to hurt you," she says. As if to prove it she gets out and walks around the car. Shadow sniffs her and wags his sign of approval.

She is wearing a gray suit jacket and a matching skirt with chunky black platform heels. Her curly hair is desperate to fling free of its tight ponytail. She looks like an art student posing as a businesswoman. She scratches Shadow behind his ear in the spot he loves. She doesn't seem to mind that her suit gets covered in silver fur. This is a good sign. Don't people always say you can judge a stranger by how they treat a dog?

"I'm Clara," she says. "You look like you could use a hot cup of coffee . . ." She pauses, waiting for me to tell her my name.

"Blue," I say, softly.

A car comes in the other direction. It slows down for a curiosity stare, decides that it's not worth stopping, and speeds by. We both watch until it's gone.

Clara studies me again. I put my hand up to my head, suddenly self-conscious about my do-it-yourself haircut.

"I don't care what you've been doing, Blue," she says. "If you're in trouble or a runaway or whatever." She sighs. "I have a job interview, but I've decided not to bother."

I'm not sure if she's saying this last part to me or to herself. She reaches out her hand. At first I think she is going to touch me, and instinctively I shrink away, but her hand sweeps past me. I get a whiff of apricot lotion. Her perfect nails are painted purple. My own nails have been bitten down, and there is dirt under what is left of them. I clasp them behind my back.

"I can take you to town at least." She points down the road. "About twenty miles."

That's a day's walk in less than half an hour. "What about my dog?" I ask. One thing for sure, I am not getting into a car with some stranger, even a nice-looking stranger in a clean car, without Shadow. Shadow peers from me to Clara expectantly, then brushes his head under my hand.

*I'm yours?* he asks. I hear him loud and clear, but Clara doesn't. I realize it's only me that understands him. I also realize it is the first time I have called him my dog.

"Of course your dog can come," Clara says. "I love dogs. My boyfriend had a Rottweiler." She pauses. "I mean he *still* has a Rottweiler . . ."

She opens the door to the back seat. "Let me just make some space." She takes out a leather bag and puts it into the trunk. Shadow follows her with curiosity. "What's his name?" She pats him on the rump.

"Shadow." As if on command, Shadow hops into the back.

Clara smiles. "He certainly is a happy pup." She opens the passenger door for me. "Hop in, Blue," she says.

I put the seat belt on and clutch my backpack on my lap. The back window is down all the way. I can see Shadow's head in the side mirror, sticking out with his nose to the wind. His mouth opens in a wide grin. I wonder if he's ever been in a car before. If not, he's sure taken to it instantly.

Clara starts asking questions: "Where are you going? Are you from around here? Why are you hitching?"

I struggle for the best answer, but she goes on before I come up with anything.

"That's all right. You don't have to answer. Not much of a talker, are you?"

I feel bad for her. She's trying to help. If I wanted help, if I needed help, I wouldn't even know where to begin. Better not to reveal any more than I have to. There's still so much I haven't figured out yet. So much I can't remember. So much that is unknown. The only thing I know for sure is that I am going home.

Clara keeps talking. She tells me about her job interview. "I got all dressed and drove out there an hour early and just sat in the parking lot. I didn't even go in." She rubs her forehead. "I totally blew it off. I can't conform. I'm not corporate. I mean, just look at me."

She reaches to her hair and takes out all the barrettes and clips to release a mane of wild curls. "There has got to be more to life than wearing pantyhose and sitting in a cubicle. I can keep cleaning houses until I figure things out." She turns to me. "You seem like a good person. You don't look like a druggie or a prostitute or a runaway."

"I'm not," I say.

"That's good." She nods. "That's good. How old are you?"

"Nineteen," I lie. I don't want her to know I'm still in high school.

"I'm thirty." She smiles, then takes a deep sigh. "Today, in fact. It's my birthday. The big three-o."

"Happy birthday," I say. "You look younger."

"Thanks." She sighs again and bites her lower lip like she's about to cry. For a minute she says nothing, clamps the wheel tight, and stares straight ahead. She lets out a series of small wheezes to catch her breath, and then she is crying. "I'm sorry . . . I'm sorry." She leans over to open the glove compartment, but my legs are in the way. "Can you . . . can you get me a tissue?"

I find a travel-size box of tissues and hand her one. She wipes her face and blows her nose really loud.

"I'm sorry," she says again. "It hasn't been a very good birthday so far. I couldn't do this job interview. My boyfriend and I broke up last night. I mean *I* broke up with *him*. It was *my* idea." She starts to cry again, and I give her another tissue. "So I don't know why I'm so upset, you know? I *wanted* to break up. But why did I have to do it right before my birthday? My *thirtieth* birthday."

She is treating me like a close confidante instead of some strange teenager she picked up on the side of the road. She smiles sadly at me. "He wanted to move in together, Blue. He wanted marriage, babies. Sheesh. I don't want that. I want to *do* something with my life first. I haven't done anything, and now I'm getting old."

I try to think of what I can say that will make her feel better, but all I can come up with is what my mother used to say to me: "Things happen for a reason."

The words sound funny coming out of my mouth. I wonder if this is what I need to be doing—if circumstances have led me here for some particular reason.

"Blue?" Clara sits up straight, as though she's just figured something out. "Do you want to have breakfast with me? There's a diner in town that serves great waffles."

I am skeptical. I only wanted a ride so I could take a break from walking and cover more ground. Besides, I have no money for waffles. How can I tell her that? I shake my head. "I ate already," I lie.

But Clara insists. "Come on, it's my treat. I want to do something *good* on my birthday. Something fun. Besides, you really look like you could use a decent breakfast."

Waffles slathered in maple syrup with a dollop of whipped cream. Orange juice, hot coffee. Maybe even bacon. As if on cue, my stomach growls. I look back at Shadow. He is leaning against the seat, having had enough wind up his nose. He looks at me with his dark, swirling eyes. He nods. *Fine with me.*

"Okay," I say, turning back to Clara.


Clara and I go to Big Ben's, a classic old diner, not one of those fancy new city diners that try to look old. There are about ten different kinds of pie in a glass case on the counter. There is bustling of wait staff and clinking of dishes and a steady hum of conversation. An old jukebox plays tacky fifties music. We slip into a booth with padded orange seats.

The waitress comes over. Her hair is wispy and her skin is

splotchy red, but in spite of appearing so haggard, she gives us a huge smile. Clara orders coffee and waffles for both of us.

"Be right back," Clara says. She takes her bag and heads to the bathroom.

While she's gone the waitress pours two cups. "Here's your coffee, darling," she says.

I bring the cup to my nose and slowly inhale the strong flavor.

"Something wrong with the coffee?" the waitress asks.

I shake my head no and the waitress leaves. I add cream and sugar and take a sip. I watch Shadow outside the window. He wanders down the street and pees on a pole. I worry for a minute that he will run off. Even though he's been with me so far and I called him "my dog," he could run off anytime. But I don't think he will. We have a bond. We can understand each other. He walks back to the car and lies down in a sunny spot on the sidewalk. He glances toward me and I wave.

When Clara comes back she's changed into wide-bottom cords and a tight-fitting embroidered tee. Any residue of makeup is gone.

"Ahh. *So* much better. I'm me again." She bounces up and down a little in the booth. "I'm really sorry, about losing it back there."

"It's okay."

She puts her hand on mine. The touch feels strange—almost foreign, as though I've never been touched before. I stare at her perfect nails.

"I'm curious about you," Clara says, "but I also have a *good* feeling. It's as though this"—she swoops her arm around the diner

—"and *you* are exactly what I should be doing on my birthday. It's strange, I know, but I think you are a *gift.*"

I have no idea what she is talking about. Maybe she smoked a little something in the bathroom. I've done nothing and I've hardly said a word, yet she's gone out of her way to bring me here, buy me food. And now she thinks I'm some gift?

The waffles arrive and I devour them. Nothing has ever tasted so good. Butter. Syrup. Sliced strawberries. It takes not being able to eat, scrounging for food in trash bins, hoping it's not going to make you sick, in order to fully appreciate the taste of something as stupendous as a waffle. I hardly notice Clara, who is still talking, or the waitress refilling our coffee, or the other customers giving me funny looks.

I finish my eating orgy, except for a few last bites I leave on the plate.

"Don't you want the rest?" Clara asks. "You're eating like you haven't eaten in a month. Don't your parents feed you?" She laughs at this last part like it's a joke.

How long has it been since my last real meal? A family meal? My family? My mother? My father? Where are they? I'm going home to see them, right? Suddenly the waffles are lead in my stomach. I blink and focus on the here and now, on what's in front of me—on Clara, on the blue checkered tablecloth, the orange booths, and the remaining bits of waffle on my plate.

My temples pound. I shiver. I begin to hear the chant. *All dead. All dead.* I haven't heard it for days. I thought it was gone.

"Blue? Do you want the rest?" Clara's voice speaking.

*Here. Now. Breathe. In and out,* I tell myself. I count, *one, two, three* . . . I answer. "I'm saving it for Shadow." The mention of Shadow helps. I breathe.

"Oh." Clara laughs. Her laugh is soft and gentle, like lilting bells, but she seems nervous now. Is she scared? Of me? Is she suspicious?

"I'll get something for Shadow. Something just for him," she says.

She puts in an order for a burger, cooked rare. "He'll like that, won't he?"

Is she kidding? He'll be ecstatic. I don't know what Shadow ate before he started following me around, but I know I haven't provided him with anything other than dumpster leftovers and trash on the streets.

"Thanks. You're being really nice. You don't have to—"

She interrupts me. "You know what, Blue, I *want* to. I don't know what your problems are or where you're from, and I'm curious, sure, but in the end I don't really care. I *want* to help. In fact, why don't you come back to my house? You can take a shower, wash your clothes, have a nap."

It's like the more Clara offers me, the happier she becomes. She sits up straighter and straighter, getting taller as she talks. A shower would be so delicious. I can already feel the spray of warm water and smell the apricot shampoo. And sleeping in a bed with a real mattress that's up off the ground, with clean sheets. I want to say yes. I am about to say yes, when I tune in to what Clara is saying:

"You have to seize the moment because everything can disappear. You think you know life, but then it's gone in an instant.

Like that family whose house blew up. Kaboom. Everything gone forever, just like that. Can you *imagine?*"

My stomach tightens. House blowing up. Everything gone. I want to hurl. I can hardly breathe. *All dead. All dead. All dead.* I want to run.

Clara's voice goes on: "At first they said no one survived, but now they think someone did. A daughter."

These are the last words I hear before I am out the door.

# BEFORE

Maybe the way it happened with Jake at the beach wasn't the most romantic thing ever, but it's a known fact that the first time with someone is always awkward. The next time it would be totally and perfectly romantic.

When he dropped me off that evening, my parents were sitting in the living room, waiting. Could they tell what I'd done? Did I look different? *Was* I different?

"Have a seat. We need to talk to you," my dad said. Something was up. My parents hadn't talked to me since I was about ten. They worked hard to protect me from everything by not telling me anything. But I was hardly a child anymore. At the very least I was a young adult. Especially now.

I plopped myself down in the middle of the couch. My parents each sat in a chair facing me.

"What's up?" I asked.

"You know I've been applying for jobs," my mother said. She patted her knees and leaned forward. "Well, I finally got one."

My mother had finished her law degree that spring and had gone on a couple of interviews. I knew she was hoping to get something big, but I hadn't thought she actually would.

"It's at a really great firm. A perfect fit." She sat back.

"That's great," I said, not understanding why this necessitated a sit-down family talk.

My parents gave each other a special between-them look. My father frowned and my mother sighed, moving her hands from her knees to brush back her hair.

"Darling," my father started.

That was all he said, when I got it. Those interviews—most of them were out of state. I shook my head. "No!" I screamed. "I am *not* moving. You can't make me."

"This job is going to give us a lot more money," my mother said. "It's a once-in-a-lifetime offer. I can't pass it up."

"What about Dad's job?" I asked.

"I can work long-distance via Internet and fax. Besides, I'm ready to let your mom do the hard work for a while," he said. She frowned at him, but he went on. "Your mother needs this, darling. We all do. You'll be able to have all the things you ever wanted."

"We've already made an offer on a house," my mother said. "A brand-new house in a fancy, modern development. You'll love it."

Did my parents know me at all? I may have liked new things, but I loved this old house. It was the only house I'd ever known.

"Where is it?" I asked.

They told me. It was a state far away, far inland, far from the sea.

"But that's hundreds of miles away!" I blurted.

"Things like this happen for a reason," my mother said. "You'll see."

"I have friends here." I thought of Jake. How could I possibly leave now?

"You'll make new friends. There's a pool and a gym in the community, lots of organized events with other kids. You could even slim down a bit if you're more active." My mother always had to slip in something about my appearance.

"There are people who like how I look," I said, remembering Jake massaging sunscreen into my back, telling me I was sexy, his hands on my hips.

"I know, sweetheart. You are beautiful. You really are. It's just that, well—"

"I'm big-boned," I said, interrupting her. "I get it from Dad." I looked at him accusingly.

"You could stand to lose a few, that's all we're saying," my father butted in. "The boys will be sure to notice you."

My father had a slightly opposite take on dating than my mother did. But I know they both thought that I was antisocial and weird.

"The point is," my mother said with finality, "we are moving."

"No," I said. "For your information, I have a boyfriend!" I hadn't planned on telling them this, but it slipped out. "And he likes me the way I am! He likes me a lot. I'll stay here and live with him for my last year of school."

My parents shared another glance.

"You will do no such thing," my mother said. "And what do you mean, you have a boyfriend? You're way too young to get attached."

There she went again. Did my parents really think I was still a little kid? They couldn't shelter me anymore.

"Your mother's right. It's better to date around first before settling. You'll meet new boys."

"I will not! I will *not* move." I felt like a stubborn, scowling little girl throwing a tantrum. Maybe I was being immature, but I didn't care. If they were going to treat me like a baby, I'd be able to act like one.

"It's already done," my mother said. "The firm wants me there yesterday. Our offer on the new house was accepted. We'll be moving in a few weeks."

"This is so unfair!" I protested. "I don't get any say?"

"Don't worry, you won't have to pack or anything. We've hired top-notch movers. The firm is paying all our expenses."

"What will happen to this house?" I asked.

"We're going to sell it." My mother sounded so cold. She never did like this old house. She was the one who liked everything new.

No one could appreciate this house or my room the way I did. This house, my house, would have a big For Sale sign stuck in the front yard. As if anyone who wanted to could buy it and live in it.

"It'll all work out. You'll see," my father said.

My mother put her hand on my knee. "We're doing this so you can have more things, sweetie. So you can be happy. You're never happy anymore. You'll be happier there, I promise. We'll buy you a brand-new computer as soon as we get there. And we can afford to send you to a better college. Anywhere you want." She leaned over and tried to touch my hair. I pulled away.

Do parents ever think of their kids when it comes to big decisions? Like uprooting them right before their last year of high school? Taking them away from the one boyfriend they may ever have? I was born in this town. The ocean was deep inside me. I'd painted my bedroom five different colors trying to find the perfect one. I finally found it. A soft spring-lilac color called Enchanted. I had the mural of the trees on my wall.

And now I had Jake. My life was finally, finally beginning, and I had to leave. It wasn't right.

# Now

I run away from Clara and the restaurant with the chant pounding louder than ever.

*All dead. No one survived. All dead. All dead.*

*One survived.*

I run in a blur, my feet hitting the pavement with the rhythm of a sledgehammer. I'm running, I think. I am running home. My parents would be so proud of me for getting exercise. I'm running harder, faster, and stronger than ever.

It starts to rain. I turn around to see if anyone has followed me. No one. Not even Shadow. I don't know if he saw me run out; maybe he'd gone around the corner to find some garbage to eat. What if he didn't notice that I left? I didn't think to call for him. How could I do that? Or did he finally decide not to come with me? To leave me all alone once and for all? No, he said he'd be with me. It's all my fault.

I stop running, not sure what to do. The rain starts to come down steady. For some reason I feel lighter, and then I realize why. I left my entire backpack at the restaurant. Everything. How could I be so stupid? I've lost my dog and all my stuff. My clothes, the knife, my water bottles, everything I've managed to find is gone. I have to start over. I can't go back. I have to go forward. Always forward.

Through the downpour I see a small white church. It sits on a hill like a castle.

The door is open so I walk in. There are old wooden pews and a small platform in the front with a podium on one side and an organ off to the other. A huge bouquet of flowers is on the podium. The church is peaceful and calm, and best of all, empty. I can hide out here for a while, dry off and regroup.

I sit in a pew and close my eyes. I erase Clara at the diner. I erase what she said. She doesn't know anything anyway. Already she is part of the past. I am here now in a church.

I take a deep breath, count to ten, let it out slowly, and repeat. This has become my way of praying. I'm not praying to anything in particular. I'm not religious. I don't like labels and I don't like things that people have to join. I guess that means I can be whatever I want. But really, all I want to be is nothing. Nothing would be so much easier than this. I concentrate on nothingness.

My breath eases. The pine-wood smell combined with the lilies on the podium makes me yawn. There is a small stained-glass window that lets in a soft light while the rain patters against it. All of this gives the place a sense of tranquility and warmth. Maybe this is what spirituality is. Maybe this is why people come to places to worship. They need to go somewhere to be calm. I lie down on the bench and close my eyes. I wonder if there is a god, and if so, what the plans for me are. Maybe this is a way of telling me to pay attention, to do something with my life. Or maybe this is what death is—not caring anymore. Not *doing* anything anymore. Giving in to the nothingness. Maybe there is no reason, no plan. Nothing.

The sound of footsteps makes me open my eyes with a start. I'm crouched low enough so that I don't think I can be seen, but I shrink into the back of the pew, just in case.

The feet walk by me to the stage. A chair scrapes across the floor, and then the pipes of the organ fill the room. Each note vibrates to the ceiling and hovers. It is a sad melody, like a long, low, hauntingly beautiful howl. One note echoes and then another plays over it.

The notes pour through my veins and into my heart, filling me with something I can't describe—a mixture of sadness and beauty all at once. Before I know it tears are streaming down my face. A hiccup escapes, loud enough to be heard. I put my hand over my mouth, but it's too late. The music stops.

"Who's here?" A man's voice.

The church is just a church again. I have been discovered.

The man walks over and stands in front of the pew so that I can't get by him. I sit up. He is wearing olive-green coveralls and has a dark bushy mustache. He looks worried. "There is no service today," he says with a Spanish accent.

"Th . . . the door was open," I stutter.

"No one is supposed to be here," he says. "You won't tell, will you?"

I must have given him a confused look because he goes on.

"Only the organist is supposed to play. This is a very old organ. Worth a lot of money."

"But it was so beautiful," I blurt.

"I'm the maintenance man. I will get fired if they know I play it."

"What was the music? That you were playing?"

"Bach."

"It was beautiful," I say again.

The man examines me more closely. Can he tell I've been crying? "Do you need something?" he asks.

I wipe my face. "I just came in to get dry. I'll leave now."

"You can stay till it stops raining," he says.

"Will you . . ." I pause, searching for the right way to ask. "Would you . . . keep playing?"

"You will not tell?"

I shake my head.

"Okay," he says. "Only because you need some Bach." He goes back to the front.

I let the music fill me. The ache in my legs goes away. The blisters on my feet no longer sting. I am crying but I am not sad. When the man finally stops and the final note fades, there is silence everywhere. Calm, peaceful silence.

The silence is suddenly broken by a bark. I sit up. Shadow? Is he here? The bark comes again. It is outside. It sounds like him —a short, sharp, single bark. He wants to come in. The man opens the door before I can get up, and a sopping wet Shadow bounds down the aisle.

Shadow! My Shadow! He is so tickled to see me, he practically leaps into my arms. I am so tickled to see him, I say his name over and over and tell him how sorry I am and that I will never, ever leave without him again. I had just started to dry off and Shadow leaves me damp and smelling of wet dog, but I don't care.

"Your dog?" the man asks.

"Yes," I say.

The man puts his hand out, and Shadow sniffs it. "No dogs allowed," he says. "I'll get in much trouble." But he pets Shadow behind the ears affectionately. He bends down to Shadow's level. They stare at each other. I look from one to the other, each reflected in the other's eyes. Then Shadow bows his head and breaks the stare.

The man still has a faraway look in his eyes. "Some dogs are magical," he says. "They know things. They make things happen. They have a power." He stands up and puts a hand on my shoulder. "This dog, he is magic for you."

I start to protest. How can a dog be magic? Besides, if he is magic, how come so many bad things have happened? Very bad, awful things. I don't believe in magic. I certainly don't believe in magic dogs, but Shadow keeps finding me and I can't explain how. And then there's the communicating thing. I look at Shadow now, but he doesn't say anything. Maybe that was all in my mind, like everything else.

"I have to go now," I say. "Thank you for the music."

I head for the door. The rain is really coming down, and the sky is dark. How did it get to be night again? I must have been in the church a lot longer than I thought.

"Come," the man says, and gestures to me.

Shadow follows him and I follow Shadow outside down a small path through the rain until we reach a one-room shed in back of the church. It's full of gardening tools, pots, rakes, and a lawn mower, but tucked in the back along the wall and under a tiny window there is a camp cot. Shadow immediately bounds over and jumps on it. I start to reprimand him.

"It's okay," the man says. "You can rest here. No one comes in but me. There are some towels and blankets." He points to a chest of drawers.

A room with a roof, a window, a bed, and blankets! "Thank you," I say. Shadow has already snuggled himself in a ball but looks up and wags his tail.

"You must need magic," the man says. He puts his hand on my shoulder. "You will be all right." Then he turns and leaves.


I leave the shed as soon as the sun is up. It's stopped raining and I want to get a fresh start to make up for lost time.

I walk for a long time on a stretch of straight road. There is no sidewalk, but there is a raised curb in front of the barrier. I take a rest to massage my feet. Shadow takes advantage of a shady spot to lie down while I finish the rest of a sandwich I've been saving since my last dumpster rummage.

The air is still. The sky is such a crisp, crystal blue that colors everywhere are enhanced. Touches of yellow, red, and orange creep along the edges of every leaf. Everything sparkles. I close my eyes and imagine the ocean with the sun glistening on the surface and the horizon a straight sharp line, only a few rocky islands to break it up. The kind of day I used to love. And if the air was at all warm enough, you could take one last plunge of the season into the icy cold waters.

I hold my face to the sun. I used to spend so many of my days just killing time. My parents called me apathetic. "Do something," they said. "Get some exercise. Join a club. Make some friends." But I didn't do anything, just listened to music, watched TV, and waited for something to happen. In the summer I waited for school to start. Once it started, I waited for it to end. I never called my friends. I waited for them to call me, which they did for a while, but eventually they stopped. I waited for someone to ask me out. I figured if I just waited long enough, eventually something would happen, and finally someone did ask me out. Was that really what I had been waiting for all along?

Shadow comes over to sit with me. I put my arm around him. "I don't know anything," I say.

He quirks his head, listening hard.

"You know so much. You're a dog, and you know way more than I ever will."

He touches my hand with his cold, wet nose.

We sit like that for a few minutes, until Shadow lets out a deep sigh and does a full-body shake. *Stop waiting,* he says.

I get up. "Guess it's time to push on, then."

There is a long hill in front of me. We must be nearing the mountains, which means there are many more mountains beyond before we get to the coast. But I suppose I am getting closer. Bit by bit.

I make the slow climb upward, then all the way down. When I get to the bottom the wind slows to stillness. I stop and listen.

I look behind. Nothing is there. The air moves in small ripples, as though it's been disturbed. Then I hear, ever so faintly, what sounds like a thousand marching footsteps approaching. I almost expect to see an army with cavalry and spears appear out of mist, ready to storm into battle.

On the crest of the hill a long line of people emerges. They are backed by the sun, so they are dark silhouettes. They are coming straight toward me. They take up the width of the road. Slowly they cross the top of the hill and start to descend. Behind them is another row and another and another.

There are so many. As they get closer, I can see some of them are holding signs. I watch, frozen, until I'm afraid they will see me. I jump over the rail and crouch behind a tree to watch. Shadow starts barking and I tell him to be quiet. He joins me in the bushes.

It looks like a parade, but it's so quiet. There's none of the usual parade cheers or singing or dancing. No floats or costumes. Just the marching of feet. Their signs and T-shirts say things like NO MORE WAR and WALK FOR PEACE and LOVE IS THE WAY. There are at least a hundred people or more—old, young, and in between. No one is talking. Where they've come from or where they're going, I don't know. It's odd that they are walking on this road, since no one is here to see them.

I watch from my hiding spot. Mostly I see their feet. They all have good sneakers or boots. Some wear little packs around their waists to carry water or snacks, but their arms swing free.

At the very end of the parade two vans follow slowly. Both have peace signs painted on the side. I imagine they are full of supplies—water, food, extra weather gear, maybe even tents and sleeping bags if the marchers are camping.

I wait until they all pass and the vans are well out of sight before I step onto the road and continue.

Shadow and I are alone again until I hear the squeaky brakes of a bicycle behind me. Before I can duck into the bushes again, it reaches me and slows down.

I notice the bike first. It's a rusty green women's no-speed. A wire basket is duct-taped to the handlebars. In the basket are pieces of computers—a smashed laptop screen, an ancient-looking keyboard, and a variety of green innards with silver and yellow wires spilling over the edge.

"Heya," the rider says. He is thin with a thick shaggy mop of hair falling over his ears and he's wearing equally sloppy clothes. He looks like he should be on a Harley instead of this funky, ancient bicycle. He certainly doesn't look like he's part of the parade. He is smiling, and even though his teeth are crooked and at least a couple of them are chipped, it's a nice smile.

"Cute dog." His voice is squirrelly and old-sounding, even though he's not old at all. Maybe twenty. Shadow does his little wiggle dance, and the guy laughs. "He could be a circus dog."

I put my head down and keep walking. He stays on the bike but pedals extra slow to match my pace. The bike wheels squeak in time.

I stand still, hoping he will give up and bike past me, but instead he stops and gets off.

As he leans to pet Shadow I glimpse a red and yellow snake tattoo curling out of his T-shirt sleeve and down his forearm. It's very detailed and intricate.

"Hey, pupster," he says, holding out his hand for Shadow to inspect. "Looks like you've seen a thing or two."

Shadow stands all perky and gives his tail a straight-up wag. The guy rubs Shadow's neck. When he's done, Shadow turns around and leans into him. The guy slaps his butt. This makes Shadow wiggle again with joy.

I steal a closer glance at the guy. Before I can turn away, our eyes lock. His eyes are almost purple, with hardly any white around them. I can see my reflection. At least I think it's me. I break the gaze quickly. Looking at people's eyes makes me uncomfortable.

He opens his mouth, then closes it. I think he wants to ask me something, but he doesn't. I'm relieved.

"Well, got to get to work." He gives Shadow a final slap, gets back on the bike, and pedals down the road. There's something kind of surreal and almost comical about him on that bike.

Shadow chases him for a minute, then bounces back. *I like him,* he announces with a bark.

"Not much I can do about that," I say. "He's gone."

It is dark when I come across a car parked on the side of the road. A dark blue station wagon, old and dinged up. Cautiously I peer inside. Empty. My guess is that it broke down and the driver went for help. Or maybe he just up and walked away. In any case, the door is unlocked. I hop into the driver's seat. I check out the glove compartment. Along with the regular stuff, there's a bunch of maps, some gum, Chap Stick, and a chewy granola bar. I grab the granola bar, rip open the package, and eat it without thinking.

There's also a fancy woman's watch. It's on a silver band interwoven with gold in a crisscross pattern. The face is small and outlined in ringlets of tiny jewels. I don't know much about watches, but this one looks expensive. I put it on my wrist.

"What do you think?" I show Shadow. "Is it me?"

For a second I contemplate taking it—I could sell it and buy food, maybe some clean clothes. And if it's worth a lot, I could even stay in a hotel with a shower and tiny bottles of shampoo and conditioner. I could buy Shadow a pretty matching collar and leash.

Shadow reaches toward the watch and attempts to put my wrist and the watch in his mouth. I pull back. "Hey, are you trying to bite me?"

He shakes his head and frowns. I take off the watch and put it back in the glove compartment. "I wasn't really going to take it. It didn't even work. The second hand wasn't moving." For some reason I feel the need to explain this to Shadow.

Shadow jumps into the back and sniffs all over the place. I crawl into the back with him. There's an old towel on the floor that I use for a blanket.

Shadow snuggles with me. A few cars pass and I hold my breath, but no one stops, and then there is just the quiet of the road in the night.

I wake first to Shadow barking and then a *tap, tap, tap* on the window. It's a police officer. I jump up and into the front seat.

Panic. Is this it? I have been found. There's no hiding now. I hush Shadow and roll down the window.

"You can't sleep here, miss." His white mustache frowns when he moves his mouth.

"I'm sorry." It comes out no more than a croak.

"There's no parking on the side of the road."

I think fast. There's only one way out of this, and that's to lie. I quickly find my voice. "The car broke down." Then I add, "sir," because somewhere I heard that if you are polite to a cop, they are more likely to let you go.

"You got a license?"

"I do, but not with me." This isn't quite a lie. I did get my permit a few months ago. "My brother was driving. It's his car. It broke down. He went for help." *Shoot, I should have said mother or father.* Two kids on the road sounds more suspicious than one kid and an adult. "My older brother," I add.

"Can I see your registration?" The officer taps his clipboard.

I reach into the glove compartment and sift through the things I found last night, including the fancy watch, until I get to the manual. The yellow registration slip is tucked inside. Before I give it to the officer, Shadow nudges my hand. I glance at the name, then hand the registration to the cop.

"Ryan Sanchez?" the officer reads, and twists his mustache with his fingers. "That's your brother?"

"Well, no. I mean, yes. Yes, that's his name. It's his car."

Either the cop doesn't notice my bad lying or he doesn't care, or maybe he takes pity on me. "Neither one of you has a phone? You couldn't call for a tow?" he asks.

"No, sir. No phone."

Shadow was sitting next to me on the passenger side, but now he stands and pushes his head over me out the window. He stares long and hard at the cop. The cop doesn't move or say anything. He and Shadow are transfixed.

Finally the cop lets his hand with the clipboard drop to his side. "I'll be right back," he says. He goes to his car. I can see him in the rearview mirror, looking up stuff in the computer. I rest my hand on Shadow, close my eyes, and cross my fingers.

He saunters back and gives me the registration. "Your brother has his license, I assume?"

"Yes, sir. He's twenty-two. He's an excellent driver." *Lie.* The lying is getting a little easier.

"And where were you two headed before you broke down?"

"To visit his girlfriend. She's not far from here." *Lie. Lie.*

"Do your parents know where you are?"

This question rolls around in my head. *Do my parents know where I am? Do I know where my parents are?*

"Miss? Are you okay? Can I call someone for you?"

I shake my head. *Breathe.* "They're out of town," I say. *Lie. Lie. Lie.*

"I could give you a ride to meet up with your brother," he offers.

I think the cop is just trying to help now. I don't think he's going to take me in. I don't think he recognizes me as anybody. See what a little lie can do?

"Thanks," I say, "but he'll be back soon. He'll freak if I'm not here. I'll wait."

The officer scratches his chin. "I'll tell you what. I'll pretend I didn't see you sleeping in this car, which shouldn't be parked on the side of the road in the first place. I'm going to drive by here in a couple of hours. If you and the car are still here, I'll have to write you up and we'll have to find your brother."

"Okay."

The officer takes off his cap. He smooths back his remaining strand of hair. "Take it to Phil's Auto on Route 36. He won't screw you."

"Okay, thank you, sir."

"Two hours and I'll be back."

He gets into his car, and after a few painful forever minutes he drives off.

I let out my breath, but my heart is still pumping ferociously.


I am walking into another town. There are more cars and more people than other towns. A lot of the cars are from faraway states, and there are a lot of fancy boutiques selling overpriced and over-fashioned outdoor gear, so I'm guessing this is a tourist town for hikers.

I come to a supermarket—a smaller version of a big chain. The parking lot is busy with cars and carts. People load bags full of groceries into their trunks. A few take a gander at me, but I keep my eyes down to avoid connection. I try to pass for a tourist.

Outside the entrance, leaning against a bike rack, I notice the funky green woman's bike from yesterday. The weird computer stuff is still in the basket. I recall that guy's dark eyes and his snake tattoo.

"Wait here," I tell Shadow. "I'll bring you a treat." I give him a pat.

He sits, already eager and ready.

I enter the supermarket and am taken aback by all the food. There are vegetables and fruits galore, a deli of meats and cheeses, a bakery oozing with bread and sweets. In the middle aisles is everything imaginable: a thousand kinds of cereal, coffee and end-less types of tea, baking needs, jars of peanut butter, household cleaners. Every single thing a person might need or want, and then some. I'd forgotten there could be this much food in one place.

First I just walk around trying not to look conspicuous, even though I am dying to reach out and take a bite of everything. I note the employees so I can avoid them. They all wear red aprons and HELLO! MY NAME IS _____ tags pinned to the front. I get a hand basket and put a jar of tomato sauce in it so I look like a real shopper.

I sneak some chocolate-covered pretzels from the serve-your-self bins. People do this all the time. I'm not the only one. I suck the chocolate with my tongue and let the taste linger before crunching on the salty pretzel underneath.

I stop in the pet supplies section and examine the dog food. I select a can with a pull-off lid, since I don't have a can opener. Liver chunks—Shadow will like that. I cradle the can in both hands and glance around. When the coast is clear, instead of put-ting the can into my basket, I slip it into the wide front pocket of my sweatshirt.

I head to the bakery. The warmth from the oven makes me want to move right in. Long French loaves poke off the end of a wire rack. Homemade cookies wrapped in cellophane are lined up on a shelf. I practically drool over the fresh-cakes display. There is one that says HAPPY BIRTHDAY, DAUGHTER in bright pink icing. I remember that addictive yet sickening taste of too much confec-tioner's sugar from birthdays long ago. That was another time, another world, another girl.

"Can I get you something?" the woman behind the counter asks. I shake my head and move toward the doughnuts and muffins. I make sure the woman is gone, then open the plastic case and pick two fat blueberry muffins and stuff them into my pocket. I go to an aisle and add a jar of peanut butter, since it has good protein, and a couple of cans of tuna. This should be enough. I don't want to take too much.

As I head to the front door I pass through produce again. It's apple season, and the displays hold mountains of apples: McIntosh, Gala, Granny Smith, Cortland, Red Delicious. I select a nice Cortland. I can already imagine the crunch of the first bite, the juice dribbling down my chin, the sweet taste. I add the apple to my stash. All the food fills up my pocket as if I am pregnant.

I turn around and almost bump into an employee spraying the lettuce. I am face-to-face with his nametag: HELLO! MY NAME IS DAN. He eyes me suspiciously. How could I not have noticed him? He's standing there as plain as day. Did he see me take the apple?

My heart races as I head, as calmly as I can, toward the exit. I see the parking lot through the glass doors. I am almost there. The doors slide open with a *whoosh*. The sun hits my face at the same instant that a hand clasps my shoulder.

"Just a minute there, miss." Dan the Produce Man spins me around. His grip is heavy, even though he's kind of scrawny. His chin is raw with red nicks, like he hasn't gotten the hang of shaving yet. "I think you forgot something," he says. He keeps one hand on my shoulder as he reaches into my pocket with his other.

I cringe and step back. "Don't," I plead.

But he's already grabbed the apple. He waves it in the air like a trophy. "Aha! I knew it!" The peanut butter jar falls onto the ground, and he picks that up as well. "I think we'd better go see the manager."

He tightens his grip on my shoulder and walks me back through the store and up a staircase that leads to a closed door. He knocks.

Inside, a pudgy man sits at a desk, his face hidden behind a computer screen.

"What?" the man asks, poking his head around the monitor.

I scrutinize his face. Not exactly kind, but not evil, either. How would Shadow react? Would he growl or wag? I can't tell. My instincts are not as clear as his.

Dan the Produce Man, who is tall and thin and much younger than the manager—a kid really—speaks. "I found her stealing." He pushes me forward. "Look." He places the apple and the peanut butter on the manager's desk. It reminds me of an elementary school kid giving his teacher an apple, hoping for extra credit.

"And?" the manager asks.

Dan the Produce Man comes toward me and again tries to reach into my pocket.

This time I step sideways so that he can't. "Don't touch me," I say.

I take out the rest of the stuff myself—the muffins, the tuna fish, the dog food—and put them on the desk.

"I was going to pay," I say. "I left my money in the car. I was going to come right back in and pay." The lie slips out of my mouth, easy and cool as Jell-O. But inside I am trembling and screaming. I don't know if I am scared, worried, or mad. I feel the hint of the trembling from inside start to creep toward the outside, and I push against it as hard as I can and remain still.

I want to break down and cry, return all the stuff and leave, but it's better to be mad. Mad is easier and safer. And I am mad. I am mad at myself for getting caught. Mad at Dan the Produce Man, who is obviously going for Employee of the Month status.

Both men are staring at me. I want to run, scream, flee, disappear into thin air along with everything else. Crumble into rubble and ash and be done with myself. But the door is blocked and my feet won't move.

"Sir," Dan the Produce Man says, breaking the silence, "why would she put items into her pocket? If she forgot her money, wouldn't she just leave the items in the store and come back for them when she has the money to pay? It doesn't make sense."

I stop crumbling and think fast. "I'd already picked everything out," I hear myself say. "I didn't want to risk someone putting it all back. I was going to pay." I even manage an innocent smile.

Dan the Produce Man shakes his head and talks to the manager in a bossy tone. "We have to press charges. She was clearly stealing. Just look at her—she's a dirty thief."

The manager picks up the can of dog food. He turns it around in his hands, mulling it over. "What's this for?" he asks.

"My dog," I say. "He's outside. He's hungry." Then I add in a whisper, so low I'm not sure he can hear, "Please."

The chair squeaks as the manager gets up. He walks to the window and peeks between the blinds. I can't see, but I cross my fingers that Shadow is still there.

The manager doesn't say anything as he sits back down. He picks up one of the muffins and fiddles with the paper wrapper. He peels it off, takes a bite, then looks me straight in the eye. I stare back, pleading inside, *please, please, please.*

He waves his hand as if dismissing me. "Get out of here," he says.

I glance at Dan the Produce Man, who is standing between the door and me. His face drops with disappointment. I think he really wants me locked up.

"But, sir," he says. "Shoplifting is a crime."

The manager sighs. "You're doing a great job, Dan. Don't worry about this." Then to me, "If I were you, I wouldn't come back in here."

"I won't. I promise." I step backwards toward the door. Dan the Produce Man has to move out of my way.

"Wait." The manager stands and picks up the dog food. "Here." He tosses the can to me. I catch it against my chest. "Take that for your dog." He ruffles the papers on his desk. "Now get out. Both of you."

Dan the Produce Man walks me back through the store glued to my side, probably thinking that he is protecting the customers from my evil ways. We get outside and he finally steps away from me.

"You're lucky, miss," he hisses, practically spitting in my face. "Damn lucky. If I were the manager, I'd abide by the law. Shoplifters will be prosecuted to the fullest extent." He points at the door as though reading from a sign, but there's nothing there. Just glass. "You heard him," he says. "Get out of here and don't ever come back."

I look around for Shadow. He's not by the bike rack. Neither is the green bike. I want to yell his name and walk around to the dumpsters, where I suspect he may be scrounging. But Dan the Produce Man is standing there waiting for me to leave. So I do.

• • •

I've been circling this town for hours, calling for Shadow. But he is nowhere. I've had to break my rule of not interacting, and ask. No one has seen a silver dog with pointed ears wandering around. Perhaps this time he's taken off for good, decided I am not worth it after all. I left him outside the store for too long. He probably thought I was never coming back with his treat.

The sun is setting. I head back to the supermarket even though I was told never to go there. This is the last place I saw Shadow. I stare at the bike rack as if staring will make him reappear.

Then I remember the green bike. Could it be that the guy with the bike took Shadow? Why would he do that? Shadow trusted him, but maybe even Shadow can make a mistake. Perhaps the guy stole Shadow to sell him to the circus.

The store is closing. I see Dan the Produce Man waiting outside. I duck around the corner before he notices me. An old sedan pulls to the curb, and a high-pitched woman's voice yells out the window about having to pick him up. He walks toward the car, but before reaching it he stops short in front of a newspaper dispenser and leans down to stare intently at something. He glances all around and scratches his head. The woman in the car screams at him again, and this time he gets in and they drive away.

As soon as they're gone I walk all around the store and the parking lot calling, "Shadow, here boy. Come here." I wave the can of dog food in the air. "I've got a treat for you." I check the dumpsters in back. He's not anywhere.

I go back to the front, passing the newspaper dispenser. I'm curious what Dan the Produce Man was staring at, so I go over and lean down to read. The front page is displayed through the clear plastic. It's a regional paper. At first I don't see anything of interest. A new development going in, comments on the weather, someone driving his tractor on the wrong side of the street, stuff like that.

Then I notice a picture at the bottom. It's a girl, about my age. Her hair is clean and freshly done up. She's round-faced with chubby cheeks and has a bland smile like she's posing for a school photo and someone told her to look happy.

The face is familiar, too familiar, but I can't figure out from where.

The article is cut off in the fold of the paper, but I can read the caption under the photo: *Girl, 17, missing from recent house* . . . It's hard to see the rest, but I think I make out the word *explosion.*

Lightning pierces my brain as I stumble backwards on the curb. My head pounds as if it could crack open any second. I squeeze my thumb and forefinger between my eyebrows so hard that it hurts, but it's better than the pain inside.

Then comes the smell. It creeps into my nostrils slowly at first, like a whiff on a slight breeze, and then it hits full force. It smells like death and flesh. I close my eyes. I see smoke and rubble everywhere. Piles of wood blown to smithereens. Dust rising from the depths. My heart pulses a thousand times a second. Am I having a heart attack?

Everything goes blurry and blood rages through my body. Burning and bubbling. Rising to the surface. Through the haze behind my eyes I can make out the shape of a body in the rubble. Then another. I squeeze my eyes tighter to try to make it disappear, but it doesn't disappear. In fact the image gets sharper. I realize it's not two bodies I see but two pieces of one body.

I suck in air but it doesn't go down. I can't breathe. I must be dying.

*All dead. All dead. No one survived. All dead.*

The lights on the world suddenly shut down, and I drift away into blankness.

# Before

I didn't want Jake's feelings for me to stop, so I pretended everything was the same. I figured if I didn't tell him we were moving,
maybe it wouldn't happen.

"Hey, babe," he said the next time we saw each other. "My
parents are out of town this weekend, and I'm having a few people
over tonight. Come. I want to show you off." He wrapped his
hand around the bracelet he'd given me. "Just make sure you wear
this."

When I arrived at his house later that night there were already
a dozen cars in the driveway. The door was open, so I let myself
in. A group of kids were clustered in the kitchen spraying Easy
Cheese on potato chips. A boy offered me one, along with a plastic cup filled with something pink. I shook my head and asked if
they knew where Jake was. Someone pointed to the backyard, and
I wandered through the sliding glass doors.

People were in huddles drinking beer and laughing. Music
blared from the outdoor speakers.

I spotted Jake near the pool talking to Adrianna. I barely knew her, though she'd been in most of my classes for years. I wasn't sure what the deal was with her and Jake. I was about to turn away, maybe look for someone, anyone else to talk to, when Jake spotted me, shined his white smile, and gestured me over.

As soon as I reached them, he put his arm around me and my spirits instantly lifted. He wasn't embarrassed by me after all. He pointed to Adrianna. "You know each other, right?"

I raised my hand in a meek hello.

Adrianna smiled a completely fake smile. "Yeah," she said. "We were in English together. How are you?"

I shrugged. "Fine."

"So, are you two an item now?" Adrianna asked, glancing from me to Jake.

I didn't have to answer because Jake leaned over and started nibbling my ear, then moved his lips down my cheek to my mouth. When he broke away, he said to Adrianna, "Does that answer your question?"

Adrianna rolled her eyes and wandered off but not before giving me a scowl.

Jake watched her, then turned to me. "She's got a total crush on me, and she can't let go. Even though I've told her it's finito like five times. I want her to know she doesn't stand a chance."

Adrianna was pretty, she came from a rich family, she had her own car, and she moved in all the right circles. She was perfect for Jake. Why would he choose me over her?

But for whatever reason, Jake *had* chosen me, and that was all that mattered. He was even willing to kiss me in front of everyone. Being Jake's girlfriend was the very thing that was going to change me. In fact, it already had.

Jake squeezed my arm. "Come on. Let's get you a drink."

We walked, hand in hand, over to Bradley, who was manning the keg underneath some plastic palms lit up with strings of red chili-pepper lights. As I reached out to take the beer Bradley offered, he stared at my wrist, then slapped Jake on the back. "You old devil. I guess I owe you," he said. "Congratulations."

Jake shot Bradley a dirty look, but Bradley went on, talking to me this time. "Looks like you finally got what you wanted after all these years." He sang the kissing song. "K-I-S-S-I-N-G. First comes love, then comes marriage . . ."

My cheeks were flame hot. I should have known they remembered me from that stupid pool party so long ago. But things were different now. Jake was different now. This Jake wouldn't humiliate me like that.

"Leave it alone, dude!" Jake shouted, interrupting Bradley's singing. To me he whispered, "Don't listen to this dickwad."

Bradley just shrugged and pointed to some activity behind us. "Looks like the band's arrived."

There were way more than a few people at the party by now. Some kids were setting up a guitar and drums on the patio. The music stopped and there was nothing but the sounds of voices for a few minutes. Then the band started. It was hardly music you could dance to, but before long, people were moshing anyway. I took minuscule sips of my beer to make it look like I was drinking and watched the dancers. It looked fun to just let go like that, move any way you wanted and not care who you smashed into or who was watching.

"Do you want to dance?" I asked Jake.

"What?"

Dance!" I yelled.

I handed him my beer, which he downed in a single gulp. We headed onto the patio where the bulk of dancers were congregated, although the dancing had begun to spread all around the yard. I swayed. Jake closed his eyes and gyrated his hips. He put his hands around my waist and made me move faster. I did. He pulled me close.

There was a charged energy in the air. Everyone and everything was moving superfast. The chili lights gave off a devilish glow, and the music pulsed through our bodies. Jake turned me around so my back was against him. I leaned in to him. I felt the *ta-dum, ta-dum, ta-dum* of our hearts beating against one another.

Someone yelled, "Geronimo!" and jumped into the pool. Others followed, and suddenly there was mayhem. Those who weren't jumping in were getting thrown in.

"Time to get out of here," Jake whispered.

We went to the pool shed. No one else was in there, and it was dark. We stumbled over some equipment into a corner. Jake pressed into me, pushing my back up against the wall. His breath smelled of beer. "You're different from other girls." He slurred his words a little as he spoke. "Even when we were little you were unique."

"I can't believe you remember that . . . At that pool party when we were little . . ." My voice trailed off.

"Shh," Jake said as he caressed my shoulder.

"I was such an idiot back then," I said.

"Nah, you were sweet. You still are."

I could hardly contain the grin spreading across my face. Maybe all along Jake had liked me, even then.

Suddenly the mood shifted and he was all over me, and fast. Pressing his lips against mine so hard it hurt and sliding his hands up and down my body. He was like a voracious wolf, and I was his prey.

"Wait," I said. "I'm not sure—"

"Oh, come on. This is what I like about you—you don't follow any of those stupid rules."

"I think you're drunk," I said.

He laughed. "So what?" He tried to kiss me again, but I turned my cheek. "What's wrong?" he asked, sounding annoyed. "You were fine the other day."

He had me pinned under his arms so I couldn't move. We could hear people yelling and screaming just on the other side of the wall.

"I just . . . I just thought it would be more special this time," I said. It came out as a hoarse whisper.

Jake let go and sat down on the bench. He looked at me so intently, like he had never seen me before. He sighed heavily. "Maybe you're right. You are too good. I'm wrong. This is wrong." He had transformed again, back into something more like a soft, bleating lamb.

I placed my hand on his cheek. "No," I said. I didn't want to be too good anymore. "It's not wrong. You have changed me, you know."

Jake's eyes opened wide—with surprise, fear, love? I couldn't tell. He took my hand away and lowered it to my side. "We should go."

When we got back to the party everyone was either in the pool or running around dripping wet. Some had stripped down to their underwear.

It wasn't long before Bradley and a few others saw us. They headed over like lions about to pounce. Right before they reached us, Jake whispered, "I'm really sorry," and let go of my hand.

Before I could respond, two guys grabbed Jake's arms, Bradley lifted his feet, and they heave-ho'ed him into the pool with a triumphant splash.

For a minute I thought they'd come back to throw me in as well, and I braced myself for it, but no one did. Jake emerged from the water in total party mode. A girl climbed onto his shoulders and they joined a game of Cherry Drop, screaming and laughing and wrestling each other. He must have known I was watching, but he didn't glance my way, not even once. It was like I was invisible.

So I left—through the kitchen and out the front door. Jake was just drunk was all. He didn't know what he was doing. He'd be himself again tomorrow.

I almost ran into someone in the driveway. It was Adrianna about to get into her car. She was completely dry. "I am so done with all of this," she said when she saw me, sweeping her arms around. "Do you want a ride?"

"No, thanks," I said, assuming it was a trick.

Adrianna frowned. "You know, Jake's not all he's cracked up to be. He's charming and all, but he's totally using you. He's not worth it."

That made me mad. Who did she think she was? "You just want us to break up, so you can have him," I said.

She shook her head. "I'm just trying to help," she said. "You are way better than him." She got into her car. Before she drove away she said, "We're not all jerks, you know. People aren't always what they seem."

# Now

The noises—explosions, flames hissing and crackling, fire engines screeching, voices wailing *ALL DEAD! ALL DEAD! ALL DEAD!*, louder than ever, and my own body screaming, all combine into something deafening. How do I get rid of all this noise?

My brain burns. I'm so hot it's like I have turned into fire. I try to run, but my legs no longer work. They scream, *You can't. You can't. You can't.*

Shadow. Where is Shadow? I need him. I scream his name, trying to outscream everything else. At first I can't hear myself, but I keep screaming until very slowly the rest fades and my voice is all that exists. I scream until only a croak comes out.

Something damp and icy covers my forehead, and it calms the fire down. Cool liquid slips down my throat. I swallow.

A voice speaks; it is different from the others—it's not coming from inside my head but from somewhere outside. I can't understand any of the words, but the voice is not unkind. A hand touches me. Is it friend or foe?

I desperately need Shadow. I scream again but now my voice is totally gone.

The fire roars back with the incessant din. I don't think I can stand it a second more; then the ice is on my forehead again, followed by more cool liquid.

It goes on like this—fire then ice, noise then silence, dark then light. Back and forth, back and forth, back and forth.

The next thing I am aware of is floating on a cloud, light as air. I am no longer burning, nor am I ice. Warmth is pulled over me, and my head rests on a puff. It is the softest thing I've ever felt.

"Hey. You're awake." Not a question but a statement from a squirrelly voice.

My eyes open to an unshaven face and a wide grin with crooked front teeth. The face is young but old at the same time. I've seen it before, I'm sure of it. His eyes are intense pools of purple. I smell mint gum, which he snaps between grins.

I take in my surroundings. The cloud is actually a bed. The puff is a pillow. I am in a room. Bits of sunlight poke through a crack in the mustard-colored curtains.

The person gets up from an overstuffed chair in the corner and opens the curtains all the way, spreading beams of sun across the room. Outside is a line of sad, skinny trees, then a parking lot with a few cars, and across from that a small white building with a sign that reads OVERLOOK MOTEL—VACANCY.

I notice the snake tattoo on the guy's arm, and it comes flooding back to me. The rusty green bike, the supermarket fiasco, the search for Shadow, that girl's picture in the paper.

I bolt upright. "Shadow! Where is he?"

"Who?" the guy asks, coming over to the edge of the bed.

"My dog. What did you do with him?" I clear my throat. It's sore and raw.

"I didn't do anything with him. You were alone when I found you."

"He was by the bike rack. Your bike was there. You took him," I accuse. I want him to have Shadow because then I'd have found him.

"I didn't see your dog. I swear. You were passed out. I brought you here."

I stare at him. Is he telling the truth? There is something about him that makes me think he is. I vaguely recall a voice, the smell of mint, a warm hand around my waist, something lifting me, falling into softness. And then soothing words, damp cloth cooling my head, liquid coating my throat.

"Where am I?" I ask.

The guy sweeps his arm across the room, as if it were a palace. "Welcome to the Overlook." He uses a formal-sounding voice in a joking way. "I'm Snake, your host, manager, and janitor all in one. This was the best room I could get you on such short notice, but it does come with a mini-fridge, and"—he pauses for effect—"a continental breakfast of delicious prewrapped Danishes."

"I have to find Shadow." I start to get up, but my body shakes too much. My legs won't let me stand and I fall back on the bed.

"You might want to take it easy," he says, putting his hand on my forearm. "You've been pretty sick."

I am too weak to fight him off. "For how long?"

"Let's see, I found you in the middle of the night, then the next day, another night, and now it's morning." He calculates on his fingers. "A day and a half."

"I missed all that?" I raise my arms and notice that I'm wearing a plaid flannel shirt over my sweatshirt.

"You were freezing, so I put it over you," he says, noticing my surprise.

I feel under the covers. I'm still dressed, except for my shoes.

"You were passed out on the sidewalk," he says. "Somehow I didn't think you'd want me to call the police or anything, so I brought you here."

"Is this . . . Is this your room?" I ask.

He nods.

The question I really want to ask is, if I've been in his bed all this time, where was he?

He seems to understand, because he says quickly, "I didn't try anything. Honest. I slept in the chair. I hardly sleep anyway, so it's not a problem. Seriously."

"I have to go. I have to find Shadow." I struggle again to get up, easing my legs gently to stand. This time they obey. I start to take off the flannel shirt.

"Keep it," he says. "It looks good on you."

I am suddenly aware of how incredibly tired I am, how my feet ache, how tense and sore everything is. I smooth the shirt back down over my arms and ask, "Is your name really Snake?"

"It's a nickname. I like snakes." He rolls up his T-shirt sleeve to reveal his full tattoo, a red and yellow snake coiling around his shoulder and down his forearm. "This is a copperhead," he says.

He pinches his skin around the tattoo and makes it wiggle. He rolls up his pant leg to show a thick brown and white snake with large blue eyes. "This one's a boa." He stands straight again. "And I've got a rattler on my back."

He looks like he's debating whether to show me that one or not. He doesn't. "I especially like poisonous snakes. But *I'm* not poisonous," he adds. "I got these in a more reckless time, when I was a former version of myself. Besides, my real name is Hector, and who wants to be called Hector?"

I sit on the chair and rub my feet. "I'm a former version, too," I say quietly.

He nods, waits.

I go on. "I'm Blue now. But the weird thing is, I don't know who I was before Blue." I stare at my feet, afraid to look him in the eye. I don't know why I am telling him this. "Where are my sneakers?" I ask.

Snake reaches under the bed and holds up my Converse. Silver tape is wrapped around the front of one, a stark contrast to the dirty red canvas. "The sole was falling off. I gave them a temporary fix. Hope you don't mind," he says, handing them to me. "Duct tape, the cure-all."

There is a pair of socks tucked inside. He must have noticed how smelly and blistered my feet were when he took off my shoes. If he did, he's too polite to say anything. In fact he hasn't asked me anything. Like what was I doing passed out in front of a supermarket wearing holey sneakers and dirty clothes, with no money or anything on me. Yet he let me stay here for two nights. He duct-taped my shoes.

Then he says my name. "Blue." He makes it sound like silk. "That's beautiful. Blue like the sky. Blue like the ocean. Blue like sadness."

We are silent. He's probably waiting for an explanation—a reason. Everyone wants a reason.

"I'm not running away," I finally say.

He nods.

"I'm going home. To the coast."

"You've got a ways to go," he says. "You're on foot?"

I nod.

"With a dog and no money?"

"Well, I don't have my dog," I say. "I have to find him. I have to."

"I'll help you," Snake says. "We'll call the pound as soon as it opens. They're always picking up strays. You can stay here as long as you like. It's nothing fancy, but—"

"I can't pay," I say before he can finish.

"Don't worry," he says.

I can only guess what that means. I'll have to pay in other ways.


Snake takes me to the motel kitchen, where he gives me juice, boiled eggs, and strawberry Danishes. I eat three of everything. I stare at the door of the lobby, ready to flee if I have to.

"What are you looking for?" Snake asks.

"I . . . I don't want to run into anyone. People make me nervous."

"There's hardly anyone here," he says. "It's not a very popular motel. I can get you your own private room if you prefer." He glances down at the floor. "I brought you to my room 'cause I was worried you could get worse." He looks me straight in the eye now. "I didn't think you should be alone."

"I can't pay," I remind him.

"Doesn't matter," he says. "Like I said, it's not a popular motel. There's plenty of room."

"Do you own it?" I ask. He's way too young to be the owner of a motel, but he seems to have full run of the place.

"Not exactly. It belongs to my uncle. He's in the military overseas. I'm managing it for him. There wasn't anyone else to take care of it while he's gone." He frowns and goes on talking. "I'm an orphan. My mom died when I was ten. My dad died a few years ago, but I'd already left home by then. He wasn't a nice guy." He picks at the Danish wrapper. "And then there was some other stuff." He bites a piece of Danish, chews, then goes on. "So when Uncle Ryan asked me to run the place while he was gone, there didn't seem to be any reason not to. I've been here a month." He looks out the window at the parking lot and the line of trees. "It's not a bad place. It's quiet."

Snake tells me he does the reservations, check-ins, and check-outs, as well as all the odd jobs—fixing leaky faucets and radiators, painting, stuff like that. The only hired person is a cleaning woman named Constance. "She's been working for my uncle forever. She's about a hundred years old," Snake says. "She can hardly see or hear, so you don't have to worry about her. She won't even know you're around."

We go back to his room. Even though he said I could have my own room, for some reason I'm scared to be alone at night, which is weird since I've been alone all this time. You would think I'd be used to it. But alone in the woods and on the road is different than alone in a motel. Maybe it's just because I don't have Shadow. I need Shadow.

"Make yourself at home," Snake says. "I'll be in the office if you need anything." Then he leaves.

I use the bathroom. There is just enough room for a toilet, a rusty stall shower, a mini-sink, and me, but it beats the woods or Porta-Johns or skanky gas stations.

There is a small and scratchy mirror where I get a glimpse of how haggard I look. I have bug bites and scratches on my cheek and neck. My hair sticks out in all directions. I eye the rusty shower. Dare I?

I turn on the hot water as high as it can go. I undress and step inside the metal stall. The water beads down my back like a warm, gentle rain. I crane my neck and let the drops fall on my face. I wash thoroughly, and then I wash again.

When I'm done I pace around Snake's room. He doesn't have much. A few books on a shelf. I read the titles: *How to Stay Sober, Siddhartha, The Dharma Bums,* a book on Buddhism, a kids' book called *The Great Big Book of Snakes and Reptiles,* which has lots of illustrations of snakes and alligators, and a spiral-bound song book of folk music.

Propped on top of the shelf are some weird sculptures. The biggest one is a kind of robot. It's made up of old electronic parts and other things. The body is a square piece of a hard drive, and the thick round head is the shiny disk. The arms are twisted forks, and it's all held together with wires and chips. There are numbers painted around the head like a clock with wire hands that show that it's 8:25. I put my ear to it. It makes a tiny ticking sound. It really is a clock. It's strangely elegant even though separately all those pieces would be useless.

The other sculptures are shaped like a rabbit, a dinosaur, and a snake coiling out of a bucket made from an old computer mouse. There is a small light bulb screwed into its mouth. I push the little switch on the bottom, and a red light goes on. I turn the light off and on a couple of times, making the snake's mouth blink red. I am impressed by how cool and clever it is.

Then I notice the motel phone on the bureau. It glares at me tauntingly and lures me over. I pick it up and listen to the dial tone. Then without even thinking, I press the numbers of my home landline.

The phone rings longer than it should. I bite my nails. Finally a recorded voice says: "The number you have reached has been disconnected. No further information is available." I hang up quickly.

Our number has been disconnected? When did that happen? Words, tiny and faint, echo. *All dead.* My legs wobble. I grab the side of the bureau to steady myself. I take deep breaths and count. *In and out. One and two and three and four.*


By the time Snake comes back I've concluded that the recorded message was because I'd remembered the number wrong. It's very likely the way my memory is these days.

Snake hands me a cup of coffee along with a bunch of sugar packets and some creamers. "Here. I didn't know how you took it."

"Thanks." I stir in sugar and cream and take a sip. I point to the robot clock and the other sculptures. "Did you make those?"

Snake laughs. "Yeah."

"They are really cool. I mean, more than cool. They're beautiful."

"Thanks. I don't like things to go to waste, so I make something out of it. Keeps me out of trouble."

We watch as the robot clock's hands tick toward nine.

"Do you think the pound is open yet?" I ask.

"Could be." He looks up a number on his computer, then dials on the phone by his bed and hands me the receiver.

I describe Shadow to the woman who answers. "He's about forty pounds, silver fur, pointy ears. Friendly."

The woman puts me on hold, then comes back. "A few dogs were picked up yesterday," she says. "He could be one of them, I don't know." She hangs up before I can ask anything else.


The pound is a few miles away.

Snake's rattly bike is leaning against the side of the motel. I glance at it skeptically.

"I was using my uncle's car," he explains, "but it broke down on the road. Right before I first saw you actually. I had to have it towed here." He points to the dark blue station wagon in the corner of the lot. I hadn't noticed it before. It looks just like the car I slept in. How strange.

"Is your uncle Ryan Sanchez?" I ask.

"Yeah, how'd you know?"

I tell Snake about coming across the car on the road and sleeping in it.

"Ha," he says. "It must be that you are meant to be here." He grins.

I wonder about the fancy woman's watch in the glove compartment. Why would Snake have that? But I don't mention it.

Snake points to his bicycle. "So this is what we've got for now. I'm pretty good carrying a passenger," he says. "Seriously. Hop on."

The seat is wide and wrapped in duct tape. Snake pats it and shrugs. "I'm addicted to duct tape. What can I say?"

He gets on and balances. "Ready?" he asks.

I stretch my leg over the bike and adjust myself. "Okay." I lift my feet off the ground. I have to hold on to something to stay balanced, but the only thing to hold is him. I falter a bit and almost fall.

"Grab on to my waist," Snake says.

I tentatively reach my arms around him and place them on his hips. We ride this way down the road.

At a stop sign, he takes his hand off the handlebars and puts it over mine. It is such a simple touch. He holds it there for a brief second before taking it away and pushing forward again.

The shelter is really run-down and smells like pee. The dogs are barking from behind a solid, locked door. It's a cacophony. I strain to hear Shadow's bark among them, but if he's there, he must not be barking.

The woman at the front desk asks all sorts of questions: Why doesn't my dog have a collar? Where did I lose him? How long have I owned him? What vet do I take him to? Do I have his health records? Is he registered?

I answer the best I can—a mixture of lies and some truth, but I have no proof that Shadow is my dog. I have no records. I don't even have a photo of him.

"If you can't prove he's yours, you can't have him," the woman says. "You can adopt him if no one claims him in twenty-four hours. There's a seventy-five-dollar adoption fee."

"But I don't have seventy-five dollars!" I blurt, my voice rising.

Snake leans over to the woman and smiles politely. "Can't you just take us to him and see if the dog recognizes her? Don't most dogs know their owner from a stranger?"

The woman glares first at Snake, then at me, and shakes her head. "Rules is rules. You prove the dog is yours, you can have him, or you can pay to adopt him, that is, *if* you qualify." She taps a pen on the desk. "There are forms to fill out. You need a permanent address."

I glare back at her.

"And just so you know," she says, "this is a kill shelter. We keep the dogs for one week. He's been here three days already."

The dogs are still barking off and on. This time I recognize a single, sharp bark.

"That's him! That's his bark!" I give the woman a pleading face. "He wants out."

The woman shakes her head. "Not unless you prove it or pay for it."

I am about to freak out. I want to jump over the counter, through the little Plexiglas window, and choke her until she agrees to let Shadow out. Before I can, though, Snake takes me by the shoulders and leads me out the door.

"What are you doing!" I yell when we get outside. "Shadow is in there. I have to get him!" I am bursting in all directions.

Snake holds me tighter and shushes me. "Don't worry, we'll get him," he whispers. "I have an idea, but we have to come back after dark."

# Before

The For Sale sign went up the day after Jake's party, and the move became more and more real. The thought of strangers traipsing through our house, examining things, turning knobs and opening doors, stepping around our furniture, circling the yard and pointing at the roof, all while trying to decide if our house was good enough for them, was excruciating.

We were supposed to get twenty-four hours' notice and be out when potential buyers came. But that afternoon I must not have gotten the message. My parents were gone and I was watching TV in my room, hoping Jake would call, when a car drove up.

I looked out the window. Three people piled out of a white SUV, a young couple and a Realtor. It was obvious who the Realtor was—she wore a sunflower-yellow pantsuit and carried a clipboard.

A girl about four or five in a purple tutu burst out of the car after them and ran around the maple tree. The mother called her, and the girl ran back and wrapped herself around her father's leg.

I could hear the Realtor giving an annoying sales pitch, like our house was a used car. "It's old, needs some fixing up, but it could be a pristine Victorian, and it's the best zip code in the state. You know what they say—location, location, location."

The woman had a large cloth slung over her shoulder. A whining cry came from it, and I realized she was carrying a baby. They all entered the front hallway. I turned down the TV and strained to hear.

"There's plenty of room for additions," the Realtor said. "You could tear down the back, add a couple of decks. Take out this wall to expand the kitchen. And of course you'd cover these floors with carpet." She wasn't trying to sell this house—she was trying to create another house.

She went on about making the attic into a playroom when the woman's voice interrupted her: "Do you mind if we look around by ourselves? We like to get a feel for a place without any outside interference."

In spite of my fixed scowl, I laughed. I bet that totally pissed off the Realtor. I sat back on the bed, grabbed a candy bar from my nightstand. Small feet ran up the stairs and blasted into my room like a full-speed tornado. It was the little girl.

"Oh," she said when she saw me. "I'm Sophie." She twirled in a circle and made her way over to the window. Her purple tutu stuck out around her. "I *love* this room!" she blurted. "If we move here, this is going to be *my* room."

I glowered. This room would never be hers. But she kept twirling and dancing and smiling. Finally she plopped onto the bed next to me. She looked at the candy bar still in my hand, then gave me a giant grin. I got another one from the drawer and gave it to her.

"It's like a magic forest in here," she said, taking a big bite of chocolate.

"It's haunted," I said. I thought maybe I could scare her out.

*"Really?"* she asked, her eyes growing wide. She didn't look scared at all, more delighted.

"Yup. Super scary, mean ghosts."

"I'm not afraid." She pointed to the mural of trees. Three on each side of the window. "Do they live in the forest?"

I nodded. "They come out at night and fly all over the house rattling things."

The girl got up and studied the mural. She crouched down and peered at the mushroom-shaped house. "They must be very small. I think they are good ghosts. They just need a friend, somebody who's not scared of them," she said with authority. She stood back up. "I will live in this room with them, and I won't share it with my baby brother. There are enough rooms for him to have his very own."

As if on cue the cries of a baby started up. The man and woman stood in the doorway. The woman shushed the baby in her pouch. It reminded me of a kangaroo.

"Sophie," the man said, "you need to stick with us." He turned to me. "I'm sorry. I didn't know anyone was here. Is she bothering you?"

"I'm not a bother!" Sophie declared. "This is going to be my room. It's perfect!" She started her twirly dance again.

The woman rocked the baby. She put her hand on the man's shoulder and whispered, "This is a good house." She looked at me. "Do you like it here?" she asked. She looked so kind and genuine.

I opened my mouth. I had planned to tell them all sorts of stuff about snakes in the basement, diseased rats in the attic, termites eating through the walls. I was even going to make up a story about a murder years ago, but I didn't. Instead I nodded.

"It's a lovely house," the woman said, smiling. "If we buy it, we promise to take very good care of it. We wouldn't change a thing."

The man nodded in agreement.

Before they left, Sophie ran back to me and whispered, "I won't tell anyone about the ghosts. I promise."

I imagined her living here, twirling around in her tutu in my bedroom, looking for the ghosts at night. She was an okay kid, but it didn't make me feel any better about anything.

# Now

Snake's idea is to break Shadow free.

We wait until dark, then bike back to the pound. Of course the doors are locked. The dogs bark from inside. This time Shadow is using his more serious bark. Three short barks in a row, a pause, then three more. Poor pup, locked in a smelly prison where innocent creatures are meaninglessly murdered.

"Hang on, I'm coming!" I yell to let him know help is on the way.

"Shh," Snake says. "I don't think anyone lives near here, but we shouldn't take any chances."

"What would they do if they caught us?"

"I don't know. Call the police or something. We'd get in trouble for breaking in, but once we get Shadow, I doubt anyone will ever know we were here. You met that woman—she won't even notice if Shadow is gone."

"I hope not," I whisper. "One cop near this town already saw me. I can't risk being seen again. We can't get caught."

We go around to the back. There's a high chainlink fence surrounding a small gravel yard where they let the dogs out to poop.

"I'll climb over, find a loose window or something, and unlock the front for you," Snake says.

I nod, glad I don't have to attempt climbing the fence. It's taller than I am.

Snake shimmies up one side and down the other like Spider-Man, and all of a sudden he's in the yard. He starts fiddling with the windows to see if he can get one to open. No luck. He goes around to the other side of the building. I wait and am just about to go around to the front when he comes back frowning.

"There's no open window."

"Oh," I say, deflated.

"There is one other way, though." He points to the back door by the yard. "There's a dog door. I can't fit through, but you might be able to."

I squint to see what he's talking about. A small flap of plastic covers a rectangular cutout at the bottom of the door. "It looks pretty small," I say.

"It's our only chance. You'll have to jump the fence first, though. Can you do that?"

"I don't know," I say. I jam my fingers and toes in between the metal spaces and attempt to hoist myself up. My foot slips out.

"Lift one hand, then a leg, then hand, then leg," Snake directs. "Use your legs."

I squeeze my calves and it's a little easier.

"That's it," Snake says.

Slowly, I move one foot at a time. Eventually I manage to get to the top. I put my left leg over the metal bar. I try to pull the other leg over, and I'm horizontal. I clutch the thin bar for dear life. I'm sure that if I move, I will fall. It's a good eight feet. It could hurt.

"Just take it slow," Snake says encouragingly. "Try to lower one leg and find a grip."

I can't find a foothold at first and wave my leg around, but then I manage to get my toes into the space and from there it's suddenly much easier to lower myself down. I jump the last bit and wipe my hands together. I smile triumphantly.

"Not bad," Snake says. "Now through there." He points to the dog door.

Is he serious? It looks even smaller up close. It may be big enough for a medium-size dog, but for a grown human, and a chubby one like me?

"It's really small," I say.

"You can fit easily," Snake says.

"I . . . I'm not . . ." I start. "Have you seen me?"

"Have *you* seen you?"

I look down, embarrassed. *No, I have not seen me,* I think. I run my hands down my sides. Has my body changed? Have I actually become stronger? Smaller? Can that happen without even noticing?

I squat in front of the dog door. The dogs are barking up a storm inside. They know something is happening. I put one arm through the flap, twist my shoulder, and get the other arm in. I slide on my arms and legs and manage to crawl the rest of the way through.

I lie there on the floor for a second. There is no way I could have done this before. There's no way I would have even tried. I listen to the barking pups. Once again I hear Shadow. *Over here,* he is saying.

I stand. I'm in a long hallway with barred cells on each side. In each cell is a dog. The two dogs closest to me, a big shepherd and a shaggy Lab mix, jump up with their front paws on the bars, stare at me with their sad eyes, and whimper.

I hear knocking from outside and realize Snake is still in the yard. I unlock the door and let him in.

"Is he here?" he asks.

I follow Shadow's bark to one of the middle cells. When he sees me, he wags and wiggles like he's on supercharge. He pushes his paws though the bars and tries to fit his nose through as well.

I open the cage and he flies into my arms and covers me with kisses. I sink my face into his neck, smelling his good doggy smell.

"I'm so sorry, I'm so sorry," I whisper. "Can you ever forgive me?"

He rests his head on my shoulder. *It's okay,* he says. *You're here.* We stay like that, just hugging, and I realize something. I love this dog with all my heart. Maybe more than I've ever loved anything.

"We should go, before someone hears something," Snake says.

The three of us start walking toward the front. It gets strangely quiet. The other dogs have all stopped barking. They watch in silence as we pass each cell. Shadow stops and sits. I stop, too.

"We can't just leave them," I say to Snake. "We have to let them out."

"You want to set them all free?" Snake asks. "What if an owner comes in tomorrow to pick up his dog and it's not here? Or what if someone wants to adopt one?"

"Yeah, but if not, they'll *kill* them. All of them. The woman said this is a kill shelter."

"They could die out there on their own, too. Stray dogs don't have much of a chance," Snake says.

"But at least they'll *have* a chance." I am adamant. "Instead of being locked up with no chance. I bet the ones with homes will know how to get back, and the others—they can always find someone." I look down at Shadow.

Snake shakes his head, but he walks to one of the cages and pulls up the latch. "All right," he says to the dog. "Go free." A little bull-doggish puppy stumbles out. It waddles like a football on legs.

We release them one by one. Short legs, long legs, curly fur, straight fur, floppy ears, pointy ears, solid colors and spotted. They fly in all directions, tumbling over each other, wagging tails and sniffing butts. Snake and I laugh, it's such a crazy scene, and their joy is contagious.

We head toward the hall that leads to the front door. The dogs are still scattered all over the place and not paying attention. Snake and I exchange glances—how will we get them to actually leave?

Snake yells at them to listen, but it's no good—it's mayhem.

Then Shadow circles around, trying to herd them toward the middle. A couple of them gather, but then they get distracted and run somewhere else. Shadow gives one loud listen-to-me bark, but the dogs don't pay any mind. He looks at me, and says, *You try.*

I stand still, clap my hands, and whistle through my teeth. A few dogs stop and sit. "Come!" I yell. Surprisingly, some more dogs sit. I clap again. "This is your chance for freedom," I tell them. "It may be your only chance."

One by one all of the dogs go quiet. Then, when Shadow goes to herd them, they line up in rows of two and wait, giving me their full attention.

"Wow," Snake says. "Impressive. You're like a dog whisperer."

Snake holds the front door open, and Shadow and I march the herd outside.

Immediately the dogs raise their noses and smell the wind. They jump around in a chaotic, happy dance. And then they disperse in all directions, running into the woods or down the road, some together, some on their own. Before we know it, Shadow is the only one left.

"That was fast," Snake says. "It's like they all knew where to go."

"I hope so," I say.

Snake picks up his bike and we are about to head back to the motel when we hear a grunt followed by a faint yip. The little bulldog puppy runs after us, as fast as it can on its stumpy legs. It's got a nasty overbite and wheezes heavily. Snake picks it up, belly front.

"Hello, girl," he says. The puppy licks Snake all over the face, and Snake pretends to be disgusted, but he's grinning like mad. "She's kind of pitiful, but I suppose someone has to take care of her," he says. "I'll call you Pity." He puts the puppy into the bike basket.

I don't see any of the other dogs on the ride back. I don't know if they'll survive or not. Maybe some will, maybe some won't. But isn't this the chance we all take in life? Survival isn't always up to us, but all we can do is try.

Shadow runs beside us as we bike. He looks up at me and smiles. *You did a good thing.*


Now that I have Shadow I have to go. The cops wouldn't be called in for one missing dog—but an entire empty shelter? The woman at the desk would surely remember Snake and me and assume we did it. The police will come, and then who knows what they'll find out about me. And that cop who found me in the car might not give me another chance.

"They don't have any proof it was us," Snake says when I explain I have to go.

We are outside in the field behind the motel watching Pity and Shadow get to know each other. Shadow is on his back with his legs in the air, and Pity is jumping over him.

I point to them. "I think they are pretty obvious proof," I say.

"But there's no way they know where we live. The shelter never got our names or an address. You don't have to leave, do you?" Snake says. "I'm getting used to you."

I know I have to keep going—my feet have begun to heal and my muscles are finally calm. "I don't know," I say. On the other hand, I am not exactly looking forward to dumpster diving again, cold nights outside, and endless days of more walking.

Snake whispers: "Stay. Please. You could work here. You could help Constance with the cleaning—she sure needs it."

No one has ever wanted me to stay. There is a part of me that wants to stay here with Snake, maybe a part of me that doesn't even want to go home at all. But it's only because I'm afraid of what I might find.

"I'll stay one more night and go tomorrow," I say.

Snake nods and gazes at the sky. "All right. I understand. I wasn't entirely serious about the job, but if you do ever need one . . ."

I follow his gaze. The sky is dotted with brilliant white, lumpy clouds. The air has a crispness to it that makes the rest of the sky extra blue and the grass extra green.

Snake breaks into his big-toothed grin. "When was the last time you lay on the grass and looked up at the clouds?" he asks.

I think back to how I met Jake. Didn't we lie side by side? But then I remember I am remembering it wrong. I was the one who got up; Jake didn't lie next to me at all. "I don't know," I say.

Snake takes my hand. I let him run me up the grassy knoll. He plops himself down, and me with him. The grass isn't exactly soft. It's a little prickly and dry. But it smells good and feels good on my back.

Shadow is enjoying himself, having a good roll, getting a back scratch. Pity crawls on top of him and nibbles at one of his legs. Shadow nuzzles her and they start to wrestle.

It was breezy when we were standing, but everything is still when we are horizontal. We watch the puffy clouds roll along. The sun warms me with an occasional peek through. This is what children do, I think.

"See that cloud?" Snake says, pointing. "It looks like an alligator. See its teeth and long snout?"

I'm not sure I do, but I nod anyway.

"Now it's morphing into a fish," he says.

I turn my head and watch Snake watching the sky. His mouth is slightly open, his chest goes up and down with his breath. We are close enough to touch, but we don't. He catches me watching and smiles.

"You're not looking," Snake says.

I stare hard at the clouds until I start to recognize shapes. First I see the fish he was talking about, with fat lips and a skinny tail fin. It turns into something that looks like a mushroom, then a heart. Then the same cloud starts to take the form of a house.

As we pick out shapes in the sky, the wind picks up and a dark cloud moves in. It moves fast. Snake says something about a sudden storm, we should go. He gets up, but I stay there watching as the cloud covers the roof, making it look like smoke coming out of the house. Then the whole house disappears behind the dark cloud. What was a bright, sunny day is now dark and stormy. A thunderous clap shatters the earth and the cloud house explodes into a million little pieces of cloud particles that rain down on me.

The burning odor of smoke comes to me. I jump up. The rain pours down, and lightning flashes up the darkened sky for an instant, followed by another tremendous roar. I run.

I am aware of my name being called, and a hand grabs mine. I free myself from the hand. The rain is so heavy I can't see a thing, but I run. I have to get away. I have to find safety. I have to find help. I have to find something. Explosion is all around me.

*All dead. All dead. All dead.*

Suddenly the hands catch hold of me and I jerk back. Snake

covers me with both his arms and pulls me to him. I hide my face in his collar.

"It's okay," he says, rubbing my back. "It's okay."

The water gushes down in a solid sheet. There are more explosions. I scream.

"It's only thunder," Snake says.

"It's more than that," I say. I'm not sure what I mean. I never used to be afraid of thunder. But this house exploding, something tells me it's real.

"Let's get back," Snake yells. He takes my hand. I clasp it tight. We run to the motel as fast as we can, even though we're already drenched.


It's dark and it's still storming. I've been waiting for it to ease up so that I can leave, but if anything it's raining harder. Snake has gone to the office and I'm alone with the dogs. I roll a pine cone around the floor in circles while Pity chases it, occasionally giving up and plopping on the floor in a frog-leg position, until I tease her again. Shadow watches and rolls his eyes at how silly the puppy is.

"Don't worry," I tell him. "This puppy is not coming with us."

*I'm not worried,* he says.

I'm still really shaken up from this afternoon and the playing actually relaxes me.

Snake comes bustling in all wet and winded. "It's nasty out there," he says. Both Pity and Shadow run up to greet him. Suddenly I want to tell Snake all about the chant and the burning ash, but he'll think I'm crazy, and maybe I am—who knows? The only way I will ever know for sure is to get home. Raining or not, waiting around here is not getting me any closer to figuring anything out.

"I have to go," I say. "For real. I can't risk the police finding me." So much for tomorrow. Now is the moment, right? I pace around the room.

Snake holds my shoulders. "Wait," he says with such clarity that I stop. "It's pouring out there."

The rain pelts the roof like nails being hammered into it. As if to prove Snake right, another flash of lightning lights up the sky, followed by more thunder.

Snake looks at my sneakers. The duct tape is peeling off because they are so wet.

"There's another way you can go, without walking so much," he says. "You can take a train."

I shake my head. "I don't have money for a train. Besides, they don't allow dogs."

"There are other ways to take a train," Snake says.

"What do you mean?" I ask.

"Train hopping is free." He gazes at his sculptures on the shelf as if thinking of something important.

"You mean like jumping on a train? Like a stowaway? Isn't that dangerous? Isn't that illegal?"

"I used to do it all the time. I know people who still do. It can be dangerous, but I could go with you. Make sure nothing happens." Snake sits up, suddenly all excited. "My friends live near the tracks. I'll close the motel for a couple of days. We can hop a train there tomorrow, maybe stay a little while, and then you can hop a train the rest of the way on your own."

"Can you close the motel? What about guests?"

"There's nothing booked till the weekend. It costs more to keep the place open than to close it. Besides, I wouldn't mind seeing some of my old buds."

"I don't know," I say.

Thunder crashes again and Pity jumps onto the bed. I sit with her and rub her belly. She's so soft, like a little baby.

Snake sits next to me. "You're really good with dogs," he says. "Like at the shelter, they all just listened to you."

"I never used to like dogs," I say, gazing into Pity's big puppy eyes. Shadow comes over and whines, so I scratch him behind the ears with one hand and keep rubbing Pity with the other. "But now I can't imagine life without Shadow. I'd have to take him on the train, too."

"Of course the dogs can come."

We sit there a few minutes, then Snake goes over to the chair where he's been sleeping since I got here.

"I feel bad taking your bed," I say.

"I'm fine here," he says. "Really." He turns out the light.

I lie awake, listening to the rain and the tiny ticking of the robot clock.

"Do you want to sleep with me?" I ask. I don't know where this comes from or why I ask. I don't know if Snake wants sex or not. He has not made any moves on me or any overtures that I can tell. He's been a perfect gentleman, but we are two people of opposite genders, alone in a room at night, and he's letting me stay for nothing. At some point he's going to expect something.

At first I don't think he heard, but after a minute he gets up and lies down next to me. He puts his hand on my shoulder.

I lean into him and press my lips against his in a hard kiss. I pull his shoulders toward me so that he's half on top of me.

All of a sudden, like he's just forgotten something, Snake breaks away and sits up. "You don't have to do this," he says.

"But, I thought . . ." I pause. "I mean, you're letting me stay here for free."

"It's okay," he says. "Really. I don't want sex. Not like this. I *want* to help you."

Funny, that's what Clara said. Well, not the sex part but about wanting to help. "Why?" I ask.

"You need help," he says. "More than you need sex."

I laugh at this a little bit. He's rejecting me and I'm laughing.

Snake goes on, "Not that I don't find you attractive. I totally do. I think you're beautiful and sad and really interesting. There's something deep inside you. It's just that it's not always about the fooling around, you know. I don't want to be that guy."

I roll over with my back to him. I fiddle with my bracelet. It's fraying. The colors are faded. It looks like a dirty, limp string around my wrist. "I have a boyfriend anyway," I blurt. "He's back home."

"Oh," Snake says. Silence for a minute, then: "He must be looking forward to seeing you."

"I guess," I say.

Snake shifts away from me and moves to get out of the bed. Now he must think I'm a real jerk.

"I'm sorry," I say. "He's not really a boyfriend. I don't know what he is. I don't even think he knows or cares where I am. He's some guy I thought loved me, but now I don't know. I'm confused."

Snake lies down again. "Do you want to just cuddle? We don't have to do anything," he says.

"Okay."

We shift so that his body wraps around mine. I stare at the copperhead on his arm as it coils around me. I remind myself that this is Snake, not Jake. Did Jake and I ever cuddle? I may not remember everything, but I'm pretty sure we never did. Snake starts snoring lightly, and I feel his warm, minty breath on my neck.

I think about getting home. It's not only to see Jake. It's to finish my last year of school, to be in my room, to see my parents. I miss my parents. They may not be perfect, but I know they care. I ought to be nicer to them. I *will* be nicer to them. But what if it's too late? I shiver.

I know the stretch coming up is going to be especially hilly. So far, I've been lucky. I've managed to find food, places to sleep. I've avoided arrest. And my body has kept going. Will it keep going? A train, I think. A train would be easy. A train would be fast.

Shadow wakes from his spot on the foot of the bed and gives me a sideways glance. I can see the whites in the corners of his eyes. "What should I do?" I whisper.

Shadow blinks. *Try it,* he says.

# BEFORE

I hadn't heard from Jake for days. I checked all means of messaging a thousand times. I even checked the mailbox at the end of the driveway, just in case he was going to be romantic and send me an actual letter.

Nothing.

I don't know what I expected. I was the one who left his party without saying goodbye. But I thought for sure he'd contact me to find out what happened. Maybe he was really too drunk to remember that I was even there.

Finally I went to his house. I had to see him. I had to tell him about the move. There wasn't much time left.

His mother answered the door. She was a nervous, thin woman with blond hair piled on top of her head.

"Is Jake home?" I asked.

"Jake's been sick," she said. "Stomach flu. He's still in bed."

"Can I see him? I'm a friend."

She looked at me skeptically but held the door open. "Only for

a short time. You don't want to make it worse, or get it yourself."
She pointed the way to his room on the second floor.

It was a typical boy's room: rolled-up futon on the floor, dirty
clothes strewn about, rock posters on the wall. More than half the
room was devoted to the latest electronic gadgets: computer,
wide-screen TV, speakers. Jake was at his desk playing a video
game; massive soldiers holding massive guns were running around
blowing things up.

I stood in the doorway. "Hey," I said.

He looked up for barely a second, then went back to the game.

I traipsed through the maze of clothes and stood next to him.
"Can I sit?"

"If you want."

I pulled up a chair and tried to watch the screen but was really
watching him. He was so caught up in the game. I didn't know
how to ask him what was wrong. I wasn't even sure if there was
anything wrong. Maybe this was all normal.

"Are you okay?" I finally asked.

"I've been sick." He swore at the screen as one of the soldiers
let out a bloodcurdling scream and disappeared in a crumble at
the bottom of the screen. Then he turned to me. "Really. I had the
stomach flu. I've been throwing up for days. This is the first time
I've been out of bed. Ask my mom." He turned back to the computer. "I'm surprised you didn't catch it."

Something was definitely wrong. Maybe he had been sick for
real, or maybe he was faking it just to avoid me. I didn't know
how to know. Usually he kissed the top of my head and said,
"Hey, babe," when he saw me. But now he could hardly look at
me. I sat in silence while he went on blowing things up. It

reminded me of the Jake I knew when we were eight—the one who was nice to me, then knocked me on the head. Wasn't this the same thing? I buried my head in my knees. I was about to start crying, and I didn't want him to see.

Finally I got up. "I'm going to go, then," I said.

"Okay." Still not looking.

I got to the door, then turned. "We're moving," I said. "My mom got a job. It's five hundred miles away. We already sold our house and everything."

He glanced at me, nodded, and gave a faint smile. He looked so sad I wanted to go over and hug him. But I didn't, and he went back to his game.

As I left Jake's house I ran into Bradley. Obviously Jake wasn't too sick for more visitors. "Hey, there," Bradley said, sizing me up. "Visiting your boyfriend?"

I raised my arm in a lame half wave, but I didn't acknowledge his question.

Bradley's eyes fixed on my more-than-friendship bracelet, and he grinned. "I didn't think he'd do it. I didn't think you would, either. Guess I underestimated. I'm here to give him the fifty bucks I owe him."

I had no idea what he was talking about, but I knew I did not like this guy. I couldn't understand how Jake could be friends with him.

# Now

Freight trains. Boxcars. Hobos. Migrant workers. Railroad songs.
Escaped convicts. These are the things that come to mind when I
think of hopping a train.

We're sitting on the side of the tracks, waiting. I feel like we
should sing some kind of hobo song, but we don't. We crouch in
silence for what seems like hours. Shadow and Pity wander around
restlessly.

"The trains can be way behind schedule," Snake says. "There's
supposed to be one here at six, but it's already getting dark. You
have to be ready to run and jump as soon as they come."

"Why not just get on when it's stopped at a station?" I ask.

Snake shakes his head. "Too risky. Too many rail bulls."

"Rail bulls?" I ask.

"They're like cops, but they work for the railroad so they have
their own rules. They don't like hoppers. They've been known to
beat them up, even shoot at them. That's why I carry this." He
takes a hard plastic case out of his pack and opens it. Inside lies a

shiny pistol. It looks like a toy. I stare at it, then at Snake. I've never seen a gun before. I've never known anyone with a gun before.

He closes the case. "I've never used it. I just have it, you know, for protection."

Just then I feel the earth rumble ever so slightly beneath us. I look at Snake, still thinking about the gun. Shadow stands alert, his ears straight up. In the distance is a faint chug.

"It's coming," Snake says. I start to get up, but Snake holds me back. "Wait till the engine passes."

The chug gets louder and the tip of a black-nosed engine appears around the bend. Chugging like the little engine that could, determined and steady. My ticket home.

Pity is small enough to fit in Snake's backpack, but Shadow will have to be thrown in. He is wagging and dancing around, caught up in the excitement.

The engine passes. The screech of metal on metal is deafening. The train is not so little anymore—it's more like a long, wild, and dangerous creature.

Snake gives me a signal to go. I run toward the tracks after him, but the force of wind blows me back. I stagger a few feet, then fall.

I yell but Snake can't hear me. I watch him run alongside the train looking for a car he can jump into. Pity's head pokes out of his backpack and bobs. Shadow runs up and tugs on Snake's pant leg. Finally Snake turns and sees me. He comes over, helps me up.

"Come on. You can do it," he says.

I brace myself, then run steadily alongside the train.

The first cars are liquid containers with no doors. Then the first boxcar passes. The side door is clamped tight. The second, the third, and the fourth boxcars are all padlocked.

"There's usually an open one at the end," Snake yells.

He's right. The very last car is a boxcar, and miraculously, the side door is open.

Snake jumps in first. That way he can help with Shadow and me.

I pick Shadow up and secure my arm under his belly like he's a giant football and hold his chest with my hand. His long legs dangle down. He's not heavy, but he's not exactly light, either.

It's really awkward to run while carrying a dog and then try to throw him into a moving vehicle. Snake's arms are outstretched waiting to catch him.

"Now!" he yells.

I swing my arm back, and with a heave-ho I toss Shadow in. Snake grabs him. Now for me. I reach. I touch the tip of Snake's fingers. He is about to grip my hand, but the train suddenly gains momentum and my hand slides out. The grip is lost. The train keeps on moving.

Snake shouts, "Run! Run!"

I fill my lungs and push all my energy into my legs. I let a superstrength take over. I am the Bionic Woman. I am faster than a speeding bullet. *Run, run, run.* I don't take my eyes off Snake's hand. I reach it and clasp with all my might while I grab the side of the door with my other hand. Snake pulls and I am able to touch the floor with my feet so I can push up with my legs and swing them over, and voilà, I am in.

I roll across the floor of the car and lie there, panting. Shadow comes over and licks my cheek.

Snake helps me up. "Welcome aboard," he says.

I start to laugh and cry all at the same time. "Wow!" I say.

"Quite the adrenaline rush, isn't it?" Snake grins.

We are in an open-air boxcar, which means it has sides but no roof. The train whistles and the wheels squeal along the tracks. This is not the romantic notion of train hopping Snake had built up. It's loud and fast and somewhat scary. Not calm at all.

"Does it ever quiet down?" I yell into his ear.

"Sometimes," he yells back. "These tracks are old."

The car is full of hay bales. We sit on one and wait.

Eventually the screeching lessens as the train maintains a regular pace straight down the tracks. The setting sun reflects on the hay, turning it golden. Now it feels calm. Now it feels free.

Snake stands on one of the bales and peers over the rim of the car. "Come look," he says.

I stand next to him. To the left I see a highway in the distance. To the right a round, faint moon is rising over the forest. With the wind in my hair and the stars starting to blink above us, I feel alive. Snake brushes my fingers and then our fingers intertwine. We stand like that for a few minutes.

"We shouldn't be in sight," Snake says. "I just wanted you to see how beautiful it is."

We go back to the safety of the interior and lie down.

Every once in a while the train exhales like a giant whale and I jump, but we are safe in our boxcar, plowing through the night mile after mile. I look over at Snake. He is asleep. He looks peaceful. At home.

At some point during the night the train stops and the last

few cars are separated. The first half of the train moves on and our section is left on the tracks, motionless and completely silent.

Eventually another engine arrives and attaches itself with a lot of grinding and screeching as we shift onto another track. I hear people milling around and calling out orders.

Snake opens his eyes. He puts his finger to his lips and shakes his head. These must be the rail bulls he was talking about. Shadow starts to growl, and I hold his snout to keep him quiet. We all shrink behind the bales of hay, out of sight should anyone come peeking in.

It seems like forever, but finally someone shouts: "Ready to go!"

The engine starts pumping, the whistle blows, and with unsteady, jerky motions we rattle down the tracks again.

When I awake, the sky is blushing pink. The train is moving in rhythm.

"Morning," Snake says, handing me one of the Danishes he brought from the motel. He's given the dogs food and water already, and they are licking their lips in post-breakfast delight. "We get off in a few minutes," he says.

We get off much more easily than we got on. One simple jump and we are back on ground as the train carries on.

We cross a dirt road, and Snake looks around in the bushes for something.

"Aha," he says, locating a flat wooden stake with a red dot

painted on it. He moves back some brush to expose a narrow trail. It is so well hidden, you'd never know it was there if you didn't know to look for it. I guess that's the idea.

The trail goes along a river. We stop and have a drink, wash our faces. The sun sparkles on the water. I feel better than I have in a long, long time. Even the dogs are happy, bounding through the woods.

Soon I hear faint music and the whir of a small motor. The sounds get stronger and we come to a clearing where a large plank is propped up by some heavy rocks. Carved into it are the words WELCOME TO HOBO TOWN.

We enter a village of rambling shacks. A man sits on a tree stump using some kind of welding tool to put together a bicycle frame. That's what makes the whirring noise. Another man sits in a rickety lawn chair turning the knobs of a transistor radio and scanning stations. He nods hello as we walk by.

Some of the shacks are sturdy little cabins with windows; some are nothing more than a piece of tarp draped over a branch or slabs of metal perched around some posts. Some are big enough for an entire family; others could barely hold a sleeping bag.

And people—some old, but mostly young, men and women, even children. Hippies and punksters are all mixed together. Most of the shacks have boxes and piles of electronics scattered around. Lots of computer stuff like Snake had, but also old radios, televisions, DVD players, headsets. I wonder if they all make sculptures out of them like Snake.

One man sits at a picnic table with a set of tools and a completely gutted ancient laptop. All the little pieces are laid out on the table like a puzzle. It looks like he's trying to put it back together. Not too far away two women are fixing musical instruments that look like little guitars.

There are a few dogs lazing around. A shaggy shepherd comes over and sniffs Shadow. They wag tails and have a playful tussle while Pity zips around exploring everything.

"What is this place?" I whisper to Snake.

"It's a community—a big family. Don't worry. Everyone here is cool," he says.

"Hey, Snake." A guy with a Mohawk stops chopping wood for a second and waves. "You back for good? Bringing a newbie?"

Snake shakes his head. "I'm looking for Onion."

"He's here. Doing the family thing with Dumpling. They're at the end of lane six." The guy gestures left down another row of shacks.

Snake and I pass more dwellings. No one is quite like the other.

"You lived here?" I whisper.

"Off and on," he says. "It was a good place at the time. Before . . ." His voice trails off and he gets wistful for a moment. I know he is thinking of something, but I know not to ask.

Instead I ask, "Is this where you got your name?" I guess this based on the names I've already heard. What parents name their kids Onion and Dumpling?

Snake nods. "Among other things. Everyone here has a past they want to forget, and no one cares what it is."

I should fit in, I think. I already have a new name and a past I can't remember. "Does everyone make sculpture here?" I ask.

"No. I was the only one who did that. Most people take broken things apart and put them back together so they work again. Then they sell them. They're tinkers."

The last place we come to consists of a sturdy tarp nailed over some boards with a flat roof to make a little square, plastic house. Some laundry is draped over the low tree branches. An old refrigerator lies on its side covered with boxes, dishes, and food. There are a few thick tree stumps around it for chairs. It looks like a campsite made from leftovers.

A big tall guy with a cascade of blond dreadlocks is sitting on one of the stumps working on something very small. He holds up a tiny gear and blows on it, then puts it back. It's a watch. He brings it to his ear and smiles.

The guy stands when he sees us and pats Snake on the back. He's not wearing a shirt, and he is toned and muscular. Even though he clearly hasn't bathed in a while, he is alarmingly gorgeous.

"Dude!" he says cheerfully. "So nice of you to drop by. Dumpling, look who it is!"

A little boy runs out from the tent. He comes right to Snake like he's about to hug him but stops short and stares instead. Pity runs over and the boy laughs and rolls on the ground. Pity jumps on top of him while Shadow noses around them.

"Hi, Snake." A petite woman with a shaved head and a lip ring comes over. She is dressed like a hippie in a long skirt and a loose, flowered T-shirt. A spider web tattoo creeps down her neck and into the top of her T-shirt. I wonder how far down it goes. I can't help staring at it. Her eyes flutter downward when Snake asks her how she is, and then they flutter over to me.

Before Snake can say anything, the dreadlocks guy grips him in a headlock and pummels the top of his head.

Snake is small in comparison, but he wriggles himself free and grabs him back. They wrestle for a minute, while I stand there feeling awkward.

Finally they stop and the guy slaps Snake playfully and says, "What's shaking out there in the real world? Who's this chickie with you?"

Snake introduces us. This is his friend Onion.

Onion says, "Welcome to Hobo Town, Blue. Or Paradise as some like to call it." He squeezes the woman's shoulder. "This here is the divine Dumpling." He points to the boy, who is now trying to escape Pity's kisses. "And this wild boy is Cracker Jack."

Cracker Jack jumps up when he hears his name and holds out his hand to display all five fingers. "I'm two," he says.

Dumpling says, "Yes, you're two, Cracker Jack, but that is five fingers." She folds down three of his fingers, then holds up her own two fingers. "This is two. Two is a good number because it is also the sign for peace."

"Tree," says Cracker Jack, holding up his whole hand again.

"Two," says Dumpling, folding his fingers back to two.

"Five," says Cracker Jack, and falls into a fit of giggles. He points to Pity and Shadow and says: "Doggie, two. Peace. Tree." Then he points to me and says, "Boo!"

"Yes, I'm Blue," I say. "It's nice to meet you, Cracker Jack."

Cracker Jack pokes himself and says, "Wild boy!"

Everyone laughs. Cracker Jack thumps his chest, quite pleased with himself. Then he runs around the house with Pity and Shadow in a game of chase.

"Are you guys still hopping?" Snake asks.

"Not anymore," Dumpling says. "Not with Cracker Jack. It's way too dangerous."

"I go sometimes," Onion says, glancing at Dumpling. "But only for a short joy ride here and there. We're family folk now." He holds up the watch he was fixing. "I'm the watch man. You need a new watch, come to me. Guaranteed to tick till it breaks."

Dumpling turns to me. She can't be more than twenty-five, but she gives me a motherly look. A look of worry and concern, care and love, mixed with a touch of annoyance. For some reason she makes me think of my own mother, and I am suddenly overcome with sadness.

"Was this your first time hopping?" she asks.

I nod.

Dumpling smiles. "Ah, the first time is so special. Would you go again?"

I start to say I'm only going home, when Onion interjects. "You got to be careful. You're a newbie. Newbies make mistakes. Ruin it for the rest of us."

"Blue's a natural," Snake says. "She did great for her first time." He doesn't mention that I almost didn't make it. "Besides, she's only catching one more ride, not making it a lifestyle."

Onion gives me a warning look. "Riding isn't kid stuff. Some punkster newbie lost his legs recently. Slipped while trying to get on, and the train ran right over him. Stuff like that makes the bulls come out in force. Plus it's a reminder to everyone that it's a dangerous sport."

Dumpling touches Onion's arm. "Stop scaring her," she says. "We were all new once. Even you. Remember?"

He shrugs Dumpling off but then smiles, completely changing moods. "Just make sure you're careful, Blue. You've got to avoid bulls like the plague. Wear dark clothes." He glances at my

Converse. "We'll have to find you some better shoes, too. You might need to run."

*I can run,* I think, but don't say anything out loud. Onion seems like the kind of guy who's easily offended.

"How long are you staying?" Dumpling asks.

"Just tonight," Snake says. "I've got to get back to the motel, and Blue, well, she's got to be somewhere, too."

"Well, you'll be here for supper, then." Dumpling claps. "We love supper guests in Hobo Town."

Cracker Jack bolts from behind the house and claps, too. "Boo for supper!"


An hour later Dumping leaves Cracker Jack with the guys and leads me through Hobo Town. Shadow follows quietly, faithfully.

"We'll check the train schedule at Cannonball's," Dumpling tells me. "Then we can get stuff for supper."

Hobo Town is even more extensive than I thought. I only saw two rows of shacks on the way in, but they go on and on.

Dumpling tells me there are six lanes that make up Hobo Town and at any given time about fifty people living here. "Hobo Town has been here three years," Dumpling says. "It's one of the longest and the biggest."

"What do you mean?" I ask.

"We're a family of misfits. People who don't fit anywhere else fit here. We all do something to keep us going. Some people pass through for a couple nights and then go back out on the trains; some settle for longer. The last town we had was west of here, but we were found out and it was destroyed after only a couple months."

I stop short. "What do you mean, destroyed?"

"Let's just say there was a mass cleansing. It wasn't pretty. Smoke bombs, tear gas, shootings, fire. Rail bulls ran us out. We had to leave everything behind. Start over."

"That's awful. Really awful," I say.

"Onion and some of the others went back a few days later, but the bulls destroyed everything. I think that's why he gets so uptight. He saw the remains." She looks askance for a second, then perks up and goes on. "So we settled here. It's way better, and so far"—she knocks on a tree—"so good."

"You lost everything?" I ask.

She shrugs as if it's no big deal. "People shouldn't have so much stuff in the first place. Most of it is useless or purely sentimental. You wouldn't believe what people throw away, and so much of it is perfectly good, or at least fixable. We find what others have tossed, and we make it new again. And then we sell it on eBay. It's kind of ironic when you think about it. I'm against stuff, but then I fix stuff and sell it to people so they have more stuff." She laughs. "At least what we make is from already made things."

I've been surviving on so little that it makes me wonder about all the stuff I used to have. I had a lot, maybe I still do somewhere, but how much of it do I even care about in the long run? I don't really miss any of it. I miss other things more. Like the ocean. My home. My parents. Jake?

Dumpling stops in front of a trailer. It looks ancient, except there's a weird shiny metal panel attached to the roof.

A man in overalls with a gray ponytail and a kind, wrinkly face stands on the porch. This must be Cannonball. He nods to me and asks, "Are you a newbie? Are you staying or passing through?" He sounds like he was almost expecting me.

"Passing through," I say.

He lets out a sad sigh. "No one stays anymore."

"We've stayed," Dumpling says. "And some others."

Cannonball pats her on the arm. "And we love you for it."

Dumpling introduces us and asks if we can use the computer to check the train schedule. "Blue's not joy-riding," she explains. "She needs to get somewhere specific."

"Hopping is a dangerous sport," Cannonball says, but he opens the door and we go in.

There is a long desk with a computer, a printer, and even a scanner, and a group of men and women working around it. A couple of guys are photographing some musical instruments in one corner of the room. One woman is using the scanner, and another is on the computer. It looks like a regular office. They live like hoboes, but they can still access the Internet and run a business. Apparently the thing on the roof is a solar panel, so Cannonball has electricity and everything, as long as there's enough sun.

Cannonball shoos the woman off the computer and checks the schedule. I just missed a train going all the way north and east. The next one isn't until tomorrow night.

"The first stop comes up right away," Cannonball says. "But it's the second one you have to watch. It's a layover. You could be sitting there an hour or more, right under the nose of bulls. You have to be extra cautious."

I don't really pay attention to the warnings. All I can think is, *I will be home.*

• • •

Hobo Town is like its own little world separated from the real one, existing by its own people and rules. Behind Cannonball's place is another trailer. This one is full of food, like a grocery store. Mostly canned goods and things that won't spoil. Dumpling fills one bag, leaves a note with what she took and some money in a metal can near the door. Behind that trailer is a large garden where we pick tons of zucchini squash.

"What do you do in the winter?" I ask.

"Pure Pete brings in fruit and veggies and other perishables once a week in his truck." She points to tire tracks beyond the garden. "That's the only road."

Our bags are pretty heavy by now, but it still doesn't look like enough for fifty people. "Do we need more?" I ask.

"No. Each lane works separately. We're only having dinner with the nine or so on lane six."

Dinner is delicious. Rice and beans with squash and bread. People chip in and help cook over an open fire pit with a grill, and all sit around and eat like a big family meal.

"This is the best food I've ever had," I say. I mean it, too.

Everyone is nice to me, giving me second helpings, welcoming me, asking if I'm staying.

A guy nearby breaks out a guitar. It's just what I would imagine a hobo setting would be like, except it's so pleasant and homelike, and I wouldn't have imagined that.

The kids take turns picking up Cracker Jack, who is the youngest, and cooing to him. He enjoys it for about five minutes and then starts whining and crying till Dumpling takes him back and cradles him. Pity, on the other hand, doesn't mind constant attention from small hands, so the kids turn to her. Shadow lies next to me and watches it all.

When the guy finishes with the guitar, he hands it to Snake.

"Play us one, Snake," he says.

Cracker Jack squirms on his mother's lap and says, "Pay. Snake. Pay."

Snake strums the guitar, then starts singing a kids' song called "Puff, the Magic Dragon." I know the song. I had a CD of it along with some other kids' ballads when I was little. Sometimes I listened to it in my room when I couldn't sleep.

The kids come sit around Snake, and he asks them to sing along with the chorus. They do, wide-eyed and happy. It's a long, sad song about a boy and a dragon who are friends until one day the boy stops visiting the dragon and the dragon cries himself to death. The kids don't seem to mind how sad it is, but when Snake gets to the part about Puff ceasing his fearless roar and crying dragon-scale tears I want to cry. But I don't.

Finally the song is over. The kids hoot and holler, then resume running around.

Snake comes back over and sits.

"You're really good," I tell him.

He shrugs. "I only know a few songs."

Dumpling is next to us. She smiles. "You guys are sweet together," she says.

I am totally embarrassed, but Snake just flashes a crooked grin.

"Why don't you go out with her, Snake?" she asks.

Now I am super embarrassed, until I realize she doesn't mean "out" as in date, but "out" as in riding the train.

Onion chips in, "Aren't you tempted, dude? Freedom. The open air. The stars. The *life*. You and the world."

I glance at Snake. Would he come with me? Would I *want* him to?

Snake smiles like he's remembering. "Sure, I'm tempted. But I've got other things to do now."

Onion scoffs. "What's a stupid job doing for you? You're working for the *man,* man."

"I'd be dead by now if I'd stayed here, you know that," Snake says. "Besides, my uncle needs me, and I kind of like running the motel."

Onion holds up his arms like a criminal. "Okay, okay. I was just asking. Don't go all hissy on me."

Cracker Jack gurgles sleepily in Dumpling's arms. She stands and whispers to me, "Let's put Cracker Jack to bed."

Snake is engrossed in a conversation with Onion and some other guys, so I go with Dumpling. There are two old mattresses inside the tent. She lays Cracker Jack on the smaller one and covers him with a blanket. I sit cross-legged on the other.

I listen to her read a book to Cracker Jack. He looks at the pictures and rubs his eyes trying to stay awake, until finally he can't. His head nods and his breathing falls into the deep rhythm of sleep. Once again I am reminded of my mother. She used to read me to sleep when I was little. She sang sometimes, too. There was a time when my mother did motherly things. There were times when we did things like a family. Times we swam in the ocean, had picnics, ordered pizza and watched movies all snuggly on the couch. Mom, Dad, and me.

Like Cracker Jack trying to stop sleep, I try to stop the tears, but a few spill out and drip down my face, hot and silent. I wipe them away quickly.

Dumpling puts the book away and starts folding some laundry. For a minute we don't say anything. I don't know if she saw me crying or not. Then she starts talking. Just telling me things. She tells me she is twenty-six and she always, always wanted a baby. "Cracker Jack's my first. I want three more," she says. "A family of six is perfect." She rubs her belly and whispers, "Don't tell anyone, but I think I might be preggers with number two."

She tells me how she met Onion when she was in the city and how they used to ride the trains all over the country. "It's a big, beautiful, wide world out there. Space like you never knew existed. People think there's nothing but highways and urban sprawl, but on a train all you see are mountains, fields, sky, and space." She gets a wistful look. "But we don't ride anymore."

"Do you miss it?" I ask.

"Sometimes, but I'd rather be here with my family. I like being in one place for now. I spent four years on the trains. Onion is a great guy—he may seem a little pompous sometimes, but it's all an act. He's got many layers to him—that's why he's called Onion." She pauses. "What's up with you and Snake?"

"He's nice," I say.

She raises her eyebrows. "That's all?"

"I don't think he likes me that way."

"There's something you should know about Snake." She puts the laundry down and sits next to me. "First he left home 'cause his dad almost beat him to death, and then his dad died. He fell madly in love with a girl, but they both loved something else more. She OD'ed in the night. He was too out of it to save her, and he blames himself. That's why he left."

"Oh," I say. I'm starting to realize that everyone has something awful in their life. No one is immune to pain.

"That's why he's afraid to get close," Dumpling continues. "After his girlfriend died, he went on a binge and almost killed himself. But he's strong. He sobered up and got that job at his uncle's motel. It's amazing what people can survive." She pauses. "Don't tell him I told you all this."

"I won't." I fiddle with my bracelet, Jake's bracelet. "How do you know if you *really* like someone or if you just think you do?" I ask.

"You feel it." Dumpling puts her hand over her heart. "In here. Do you feel it?"

"I'm not sure." I do feel something when I'm with Snake, and after what Dumpling just told me, I'm totally sad for him. He lost everyone. But what about me? How can I trust my feelings when I don't even know who I am or what's happened?

"You two connect, I can tell," Dumpling says. "But sometimes you're the last to know if it's real or not. I didn't know with Onion right away. It takes time to trust."

"I don't have time," I say.

"There's always time," she says. "Besides, you don't have to run away."

"I'm not," I say. "I'm going home." The word *home* feels weird on my tongue, like it's a word that no longer belongs there. I expect my stomach to tighten, but it doesn't.

"Really?" says Dumpling. "That's so sweet. You're not running away, you're running home. You're not trying to start over. You're returning." She says this as a fact, not a question. She may be right. I hadn't thought about it that way.

"You know what they say, though?" she asks.

I shake my head.

"You can't ever go back. Not really."

# Before

Mom and Dad had been arguing all week, but on the morning of moving day my mother was a force to reckon with. When she was in panic mode it was wise to steer clear.

"Careful with that couch, one of the legs is wobbly!" she yelled at the movers, then at my father, "I *told* you we should've gone with the other company."

"It'll be fine." My father tried to calm her down but only made it worse.

I snuck upstairs so she couldn't start in on me. I went into my empty room and lay down smack in the center. I stared at the tree mural and the mushroom house. I wished I could move in there and never leave.

An August breeze rolled through the open window, warm and salty, carrying the call of gulls. I had imagined bringing Jake up to my room. I wanted him to come in right then, stand over me and ask if I was dead or asleep. I'd say neither. He'd lie on the floor next to me, wrap his arms around me and call me babe, tell me that he'd miss me like crazy and he'd come visit.

I checked the loose floorboard where I kept my secret stash. There were still three chocolate bars there. I ate two and was about to down the third when I heard footsteps in the hall. Jake! I waited for him to come bounding in, full of smiles and love. But it was only my father.

"It's time to go," he said.

I trudged down the stairs. *Come on, Jake,* I pleaded. I clasped my "more-than-friendship" bracelet. *This is your last chance. Where are you? Please, please, please.*

And lo and behold, when I got outside, there he was, walking up the driveway. At first I thought I must be seeing things. I blinked. It really was him. He'd heard my plea.

My mother was rearranging some things in the car; if she saw him, she didn't say anything. When Jake reached me I led him behind the maple tree. We stood face-to-face.

"We're moving," I said, as if it were brand-new news. "Will you visit?" I was afraid I was sounding desperate, but I didn't care.

"I . . . I don't know." He kicked the dirt. "Look, I'm really sorry. I can't do this."

"What?" I asked. "Can't do what? Did I do something?" I held my breath.

"No," he said. "I don't think so. I mean no, you didn't. I'm totally screwed up."

"Was it the party? I should've stayed."

"That's not it."

"Then what?"

"It was supposed to be a joke. A stupid bet. It was Bradley's idea, but I went along with it."

What did he mean, it was Bradley's idea? What was a bet? Dating him? The bracelet? Everything? Is that what Bradley meant when he said he owed Jake money?

"Forget about me," he said.

"I don't want to forget about you," I said. He looked so vulnerable. I was more confused than ever. I rubbed the bracelet between my fingers. Jake wouldn't do something like this.

"You should." He took my hand. "But I want you to know, even though it started out as a bet, I *did* like you. That's why I couldn't keep going with it. And that's why you should forget it." He dropped my hand, leaving it cold, and then walked away. Just like that.

This was so, so much worse than swatting me with a swim noodle. I thought about running after him. I was about to when my father came out of the house.

"We've got to go," he said. "We've got a long trip ahead of us."

I got into the car and we pulled away. I watched as Jake got smaller and smaller until he turned at the end of the street.

I glanced toward my bedroom window. I tried to imagine what it would be like for some other girl to live there, twirling in circles, dancing around and around my enchanted room.

I felt like I'd just lost everything I'd ever known.

# Now

Snake and I sleep in an empty tent in lane six. We go to sleep holding hands. When I wake up, Snake is propped on his elbow watching me.

"Hey," I whisper.

"Hey," he whispers. "I have to go back to the motel now," he says. "Will you be all right?" I think about him being afraid to get too close to anyone. I am afraid, too.

As if on cue Shadow comes into the tent and nuzzles me. "I guess so," I say.

"You're lucky you have Shadow," Snake says. "You two are symbiotic."

Shadow cocks his head, nods. *Yes. You are lucky.*

"You have Pity," I say, just as Pity comes scurrying in after Shadow and stretches her stumpy legs.

Snake picks her up, rocks her until she squirms, and puts her down again. He takes something from his backpack. "I made this for you."

It's a robot clock, like the one in his room only much smaller. A watch piece makes its face and tiny springs stick out for arms and legs. It works, too. It's the same watch I tried on the night in the car. I laugh to think I almost was going to take this watch and now he's giving it to me.

"It's beautiful," I say. "Thank you." I put it in my pocket.

He holds out something else. It's the gun case. "Do you want this?"

I take a few steps back.

"It's dangerous out there. You might need it." He opens the case, picks up the gun, and holds it out on his palm, the way you'd offer a carrot to a horse.

"It's so small." I take the pistol, turn it over in my hands, feeling its weight. It's heavier than it looks. "This could really kill someone?" I ask.

"If you're close enough and have good aim. It can certainly maim something pretty bad."

"Is it loaded?" I ask.

"It's in lock mode, so it can't go off."

I hold the gun to my temple. Touch the metal barrel against my skin. For such a small object it has a lot of power. I close my eyes and imagine nothingness.

"Don't *do* that!! Don't ever do that!" Snake pulls my hand down.

Shadow whines at my side.

I open my eyes. "I thought you said it was locked."

"It doesn't matter. Don't *ever* point a gun at anything unless you plan to shoot it," Snake says.

My mind flickers back to the homeless guy, Jimbo, with the

knife. What if I'd had a gun? If I shot him, I'd be a murderer. What if I had a gun that night in the woods when I saw the animal? Maybe I could have had it for supper. What if I'd pulled a gun on the cop who found me in the car? Or what if I am lying in the woods or on a bench in the middle of the night and I have a panic attack and the gun is right there? So simple. Maybe too simple.

I give the gun back to Snake and shake my head. "Thanks, but I can't."

He puts it away. "I just want you to be safe. I care about you." He pauses, then says, "I like you, Blue. I like you a lot, but the timing's just not right. I still need to figure some stuff out."

I am happy, sad, and relieved all at the same time. I'm happy because he likes me. A lot! I'm sad because we have to say goodbye when we are just getting to know each other. I'm relieved because, well, because I want to like Snake, too. I *do* like him, but I can't really know for sure. Not now. I have some stuff to figure out, too. "I know," I say. "Me, too."

"If we're supposed to see each other again, we will," he says. "You never know what the future holds. Distances aren't as far as you think." He takes two cards from his pocket and gives them to me. "Here's my address and the number at the motel. The other is a phone card. There's still money on it. Call me anytime you want." He takes off his flannel, so he's just in his T-shirt, and wraps it around my shoulders. "Take this, too. It might get cold."

I place my hand on his and clutch it tight. Suddenly I want to scream in his arms. *I am so lost! Something awful has happened!* But I sense that he already knows this. Maybe because he is lost, too.

We stand there for a second in silence, and then he moves closer and we hug.

I bite my lip to keep it from trembling. It doesn't work. Snake places his finger over my mouth gently and whispers my name. Then we kiss.

I definitely feel something, something maybe worth living for, and I forget everything else.

"We'll see each other again," he says when we break apart.

I touch my fingers to my lips, feeling the warmth that lingers there.


Snake has gone, the day is over, and it is time for me to say good-bye to Dumpling, Onion, Cracker Jack, and everyone else at Hobo Town. Dumpling loads me with a pack of food—dried fruit and sandwiches. Someone found a pair of boots that fit me perfectly, and my feet are snug and cradled. How ironic that I am no longer walking.

"Come back anytime," Dumpling says, pulling me into a hug. "If you need to or just want to. You are always welcome at Hobo Town."

"Thanks," I say. I want to say more. I want to tell her that in the last two days I have felt safer, more comfortable, and maybe even happier than I have since . . . since I started. Maybe since even before. But I just hug her back and head down to the tracks for my next ride home.

Shadow and I wait. It's not late this time, but when the train comes the only boxcar with an open door is barely wide enough for us to squeeze through. I throw Shadow in first and then push myself up. My foot catches on a metal hinge that juts out, but I make it.

This car is smaller than the one I rode with Snake, and it's full of concrete slabs. Shadow and I squish in between them and sit on the cold, hard floor.

The night is overcast and an almost full moon weaves in and out of heavy clouds. The train splits my ears with its roaring and screeching. The wind whips in through every open crack. I pull up my hood and wrap Snake's flannel shirt around me. Shadow nudges under my upright knees, and I hug him close. We share a sandwich, but Shadow keeps his radar ears alert even while eating.

We haven't gone that far when the train slows and stops. We must be at the station already.

I hear shouting—deep men's voices—and feet crunching on gravel. Beams from a flashlight dart around the sky. The voices are rushed and taunting like playground bullies, but more menacing.

"Come out, come out, wherever you are. Hello, hello, hello?"

I remember the warnings: *Rail bulls have guns, and they're not afraid to use them.* Why didn't I take Snake's pistol after all?

I try to still my thumping heart. Shadow gets up and paces in the narrow car. His ears twist and turn. The footsteps are getting closer, until they stop right next to our car, and I can see a shadowy figure through the opening. I suck in my breath.

A light shines in and spirals over and around the concrete blocks. It hits Shadow, radiating him for an instant before passing. Then the light backtracks onto him and stays there.

"What have we here?" a voice asks.

Shadow curls his lip and snarls. His teeth glisten. He glows like a ghost dog. But the man doesn't look at Shadow. He swirls his flashlight around until it finds me and stops. I am blinded. I cannot see a thing. This is not good.

"Well, well, well . . ." The voice is gruff. "It's our lucky night. A stowaway."

He yells to his cohorts that he's found one.

I move fast—up and out the door, screaming for Shadow to follow. I land on my feet and start running. The rail bull reaches to stop me and catches my sleeve. I slide myself out of it and keep running, leaving him holding Snake's flannel shirt.

I hear Shadow behind me, growling fiercely, and the man screams, "Goddamn dog!"

Shadow must have bitten him. *Good dog,* I think. I keep running. There are more voices and footsteps, lights shining, more men behind me.

I keep running.

Shadow is beside me now. We head to the woods. Wet pine needles crunch beneath my feet. It's easier to run on than the gravel, and I am swift in the sturdy boots.

The men trail behind—their voices are harder to make out now, so I ease my pace and begin to relax. Then my foot hits something—a root, a rock. I attempt to steady myself, but I am a second too late and I meet the ground with a sudden *thunk.* There is a cracking sound, like a branch snapping in two but louder. The impact is harder than I expected. I cannot believe I have allowed myself to fall. I expect to get up, wipe off the leaves and dirt, and keep moving. I use my arms to push, and instantly I know something is wrong.

Terribly wrong.

Pain sears through my right shoulder all the way down my arm. I want to scream bloody hell, but I know the rail bulls are still out there and could be gaining on me.

I prop myself up on my good arm and stare at the other. It is soft and limp and hangs off my body like some foreign append-age. But the pain tells me it is still attached. It is far too difficult to stand. I inch behind a mound of earth, screaming in my head with each move and hoping the sound isn't actually coming out of my mouth. I lie as still as possible trying to disappear into the dark.

Shadow nudges my neck gently. *Everything will be okay.*

But how does he know?

We stay there motionless. All is silent, but I know it's not over. Sure enough, a second later there is some snapping of sticks, a shuffle of leaves. Shadow's hackles rise, and suddenly he runs off.

The next thing I hear is barking. Ferocious snarls and growls. It is Shadow, but he is fiercer than I could ever imagine. He is out for blood.

"Oh, crap," says one of the bulls. His voice is close, too close.

"Shoot the thing," another one says. "It's gone mad."

Everything in my brain sends out a screaming *No!,* but words are not able to leave my body.

And then a hard *craaaack* splits the night. The shot reverber-ates all around the trees, turns to a loud ringing, and then slowly fades until there is nothing.

My heart stops. Everything is silent. There is no more barking.

A gruff voice breaks the quiet. "What happened?"

It is followed by a low growl. Shadow's growl!

Relief swoops through me.

Another rail bull says, "My hand . . . It slipped. It was a clear shot and I missed."

"Try again."

"No way. That dog's possessed. It's bad luck to kill something possessed. I got it to back off."

"But you didn't even scare it—it's standing right there. Look at its eyes. It's not a dog, it's a monster."

"Exactly. Come on, let's get out of here."

"But the stowaway?"

"We got her off the train. She's probably just a runaway from that hippie place." Slowly the rail bulls start to walk away, but I can still hear them. "It's been there for years, got a name and everything. Hobo Town. Isn't that a gas? That's where all the hoppers come from."

"Why don't we get rid of it, then?"

"How?"

Their voices are barely audible now. But I think I hear one of them say, "A can of gasoline, a couple of matches. And poof. They're gone. No more Hobo Town."

I keep my breath shut tight inside my lungs until I hear the train squeal away. Only then do I allow myself to breathe and to register what they said, but it can't be true. I am hearing things. I close my eyes. All I feel is pain. Nothing else seems real. I want to take my arm off, rise up out of my body, and leave it all there.

"Shadow," I manage. He comes to me, licks my nose gingerly.

I exhale into his fur. "Shadow." I'm not sure if I'm saying this out loud or only in my head. "Help."

Shadow barks but I can't understand what he's trying to say. He turns and walks off into the woods. I watch him until he is nothing more than a ghostly shape.

I am alone in the silent night.


I go in and out of awareness. Shadow has left. I must be dying. Seventeen years old—I should be in the prime of my life, surrounded by family and friends, smiling and laughing every day, playing sports, singing in the school choir, studying for SATs, and dreaming about getting into a good college. Was I ever like that? I let everything pass me by, just waiting for something else. Never living.

And now I am lost in the woods, my body in pain. Alone. Alone. Alone.

If a tree falls in the woods when no one is there, does it still make a noise? If a girl dies in the woods when no one is there, does anyone care? If no one knows I am here, do I even exist?

*All dead. All dead. All dead.* Including me, once and for all.

Time passes but I don't know how much. Is it minutes, hours, days?

Then from somewhere I hear Shadow's single bark. And another. Maybe I am not dead yet. Feet crunch through the pine needles. Not just Shadow's but another set following. A human. Are the rail bulls still out there? Did they find Shadow again?

Shadow reaches me, touches me with his snout. *I brought help,* he says.

A woman crouches next to me, and silver silk hair wisps across my cheek. I stare into a face creased with wrinkles. Is she a witch? Good or bad? She must be good if Shadow brought her.

"Can you sit?" the woman asks. She helps prop me up on my good arm. "I'm here to help," she says calmly. She takes my sore arm in both hands.

I wince with pain.

She rubs my palm and forearm. "You've dislocated your shoulder. I can fix it." She lifts my hand, tucks it under her arm, and shifts closer. "This will hurt, but it will be over before you know it. Try to distract yourself," she says. "Tell me about something good."

I don't say anything. There is nothing good.

"Tell me about your dog. What's his name?" she asks.

"Shadow," I whisper.

"Do you know what kind he is?"

I shake my head.

"He looks like he could be part wolf," she answers for me.

"I guess," I say.

"Or part ghost. How long have you had him?"

Before I can respond, she grabs my arm in one swift move and yanks it toward her. I hear a popping sound, then the eruption of my own voice howling through the trees.

"That's it," she says. "Breathe. Scream." She keeps pulling.

I howl louder.

She eases my arm down to my side, and all of a sudden it's

over. My arm is no longer foreign. It is back to being my arm again.

I shake it out and use it to wipe my face. "What did you do?" I ask the woman.

"Your humerus separated from your scapula," she says. "I rotated it back into place. Best to keep it still; it'll be sore for a few hours. But you should be back to normal in no time."

"Thank you," I say.

"I live nearby," the woman explains. "I heard barking and your dog was outside. He led me here."

I look at Shadow. Here I thought he'd gone and abandoned me, but it was just the opposite—he'd gone and saved me. I feel guilty for even thinking he'd leave me there to die. I scratch his chin.

*I would never leave you.*

"My name is Eudora," the woman says, helping me to stand. "You should rest. I'll take you to my cabin and fix you a cup of tea."

We follow a narrow path through the woods. The woods are not so menacing now as the sun begins to rise. Everything looks better in the daylight.


Eudora's cabin sits by itself nestled in the trees. There is a dirt road behind it with a truck parked. The building is small but sturdy —it looks like it's been there for years. There are stacks of books on every surface, books covering the couch, books scattered across the floor. There's a small alcove with a bed, and that, too, is oozing with books.

Shadow's tail perks straight with excitement as he sniffs the air. *Oh, she's got cats!* He chases two cats across the room and under the bed.

"Shadow," I say sternly. "Stop that."

He eyes me. *But they're cats.*

"Don't worry about it," Eudora says. "They're tough. He just wants to play."

The cats peer from their hiding place. One of them steps out and pokes Shadow with its paw. Shadow sniffs it, decides it's not going to play, and lumbers off to drink some water from the bowl Eudora has filled for him.

Eudora points to the couch and tells me to sit. I don't know if I should move the books or sit on top of them, so I remain standing.

"Oh, sorry," she says, and picks up an armload from the couch. She turns around looking for a place to put them and finally sets them on the floor next to some others. "Too many books," she says, "but they are one thing I can't get rid of. Everything else was easy— useless knickknacks, fancy dishes, even photographs. But books . . . well, I couldn't do it. When I'm dead and gone someone can donate them to a library or use them for kindling." She laughs.

I sit in the cleared spot on the couch while she puts on a kettle. I pick up a book from the pile and flip through. It's poetry—all about nature.

Eudora comes over with a thick candle and a little bottle of liquid and sets it on the table. "'I believe a leaf of grass is no less than the journey work of the stars.'" She points to the book. "That's Walt Whitman, *Leaves of Grass.* One of my favorites."

She pours a few drops of the liquid onto the candle and lights it. The room fills with the aroma of lavender. "This will put healing energy in the air," she says. The kettle whistles and she goes to the stove. Shadow rests his head in my lap and sighs. I stroke his nose.

"You've got a special dog there," Eudora says, handing me a mug of peppermint tea. "He saved your life."

I take a sip. The sweet peppermint, the lavender incense, the coziness of all her books—it relaxes me. Makes me want to close my eyes, drift into a warm, safe sleep.

But Eudora is watching. It seems like she is waiting for me to say something. So I ask, "How did you know how to fix my shoulder?"

"I was a nurse," she says. "But I never fit into society. So I built this place. I have everything I need here. I have my books and my writings. And it's quiet." She pats my good shoulder. "Now tell me what you're doing out here wandering around in the night with a dislocated shoulder."

What do I say? I don't know if I have any more lies left, but then I'm not certain of the truth either. "I don't remember everything," I finally admit, "but I'm going home. I'm almost there."

"Do you remember your name?" she asks.

"I'm Blue," I say. "At least, I am now."

"Do you remember where you live?"

"On the ocean. In a yellow house with green shutters." The second I say this I wish I hadn't.

"Are your parents waiting for you?"

"I . . . I don't know. I have to tell them I'm sorry." I start to feel sick.

The woman tips her head and her eyebrows rise, as though she suddenly recalls something. Then she inhales quickly and her face softens. "You're . . . you're that girl, aren't you?"

"What girl?" I ask. My body tenses. My shoulder begins to throb.

"The one in the news. I read about you. You used to live on the coast, then you moved."

How does she know this? What does she mean, *used to*? What does she mean, *moved*?

She goes on. "People are looking for you. They know you didn't die." Her voice fades. Her mouth continues to move in the shape of words, but the sound is muffled and I can no longer hear. I close my eyes so I don't have to see her mouth. I wait for the chant to take over. I wait for the nausea. I wait for panic, but it doesn't come. Shadow noses me. I open my eyes and pet him. Then I can hear again, and she is saying something else.

"Never mind. I'm wrong. I don't know what I was thinking." She puts her hand on my back.

I look at her. "I have to go," I say, even though my mind is all fuzzy.

"No," Eudora says, as though leaving on my own is not an option. "You're in no condition. You'll stay here and rest."

I start to protest.

She holds up her hand. "I'm going to say something, Blue, and you tell me if you think it's true. This is what I think. I think something happened and it was so awful that you have shut it out. You've lost parts of your memory." She pauses. "Does that make any sense?"

"You mean I have amnesia?" I ask. "Like I hit my head and forgot everything?"

"Could be, but there are other ways people lose memory. Sometimes it's caused by a blow to the head, or sometimes it's a traumatic event that the brain erases in order to survive. Sometimes it's all memory that is lost, sometimes just bits and pieces."

I let this information sink in, then ask, "Will I ever remember everything?" I'm not sure I want to.

Eudora studies me carefully. "'All truths wait in all things. They neither hasten their own delivery nor resist it.'" She pauses. "Whitman, again. You can't push the mind to remember things it's not ready to remember. It'll come back when you're ready. You must not be ready yet. Do you remember what just happened— out in the woods before I came?"

"Yes," I say. "I got a train, I almost got caught." I start to tell her about the rail bulls chasing me, but then stop as I suddenly recall their conversation in the woods. I thought it had been my imagination, but I now hear their voices loud and clear: "A can of gasoline, a couple of matches. And poof. No more town." It dawns on me—they are going to burn down Hobo Town!

I have to warn Dumpling and Onion, and everyone! The whole town, everything in their lives will be destroyed; they could die. I'm so close to my own home, but I can't let theirs burn down.

Eudora is still talking but I tune her out again. All I can think about is getting to Hobo Town in time. I can't up and flee. Eudora means well, but she will call someone for sure—she will try to stop me.

"Okay, I'll stay here," I tell her.

"Good. That's good. Tomorrow your arm will be much better, you'll see. I'll drive you wherever you want to go."

But I know that won't happen. I will sneak out as soon as I can and head backwards.

Finally Eudora falls asleep. I sneak out of her wonderfully warm home, full of lavender, peppermint, and poetry. Instead of heading home, I am retracing my steps. I am going in the wrong direction.

I have no choice. I remember little Cracker Jack holding up his fingers and calling himself wild boy. They can't burn his home down. They can't. I only hope I'm not too late.

Shadow leads the way back through the woods to the train tracks, and we follow them west. The bulls found me on the second stop, so Hobo Town can't be more than fifteen or twenty miles. Still, it will take me all day to get there.

I run for a bit, then slow to a fast walk. It's so much easier in the boots. I imagine the boots themselves are giving me the encouragement I need. *Go, go, go. We've got you covered.* This time I watch the ground in front of me. I won't fall.

The sun rises to its full height and gleams down on me. I hear a train whistle, and I turn into the woods well before the train passes. If the bulls catch me a second time, they'll kill Shadow for sure and probably me, too. The train whizzes by heading east. I watch until it is out of sight.

I run. I walk. I rest. I run again. I drink water. I eat some of the food Dumpling gave me. The hours go by. I stay steady. I stay focused. I can't be too late, I just can't.

. . .

By the time the sun has crossed to the other side of the sky and started to set, I know I am close. I recognize the spot where I hid out waiting to catch the train.

In the approaching darkness I make out the shape of a small person crouched on the track. Shadow reaches the person first. He's not growling or barking, so it must be all right.

As I get closer I see that it is a child, a boy. The boy hugs Shadow around the neck and sings, "Doggie-do, doggie-do, doggie-do" over and over.

"Cracker Jack!" I yell. When I reach him I squeeze him tight.

"Ow." He wriggles out of my grip. It takes him a second to register me. "Yello, Boo," he says.

"Cracker Jack." I keep my hand on his shoulder, afraid he might disappear if I don't hold on to him. "What are you doing here? Where is everyone else?"

His eyes open wide. He looks scared. It's the look of something bad. I *am* too late. The bulls came. They burned down everything.

*All dead. All dead. All dead.*

I hug Cracker Jack tight. I will hold him forever if I have to. But he won't let me. He squirms away and points to himself. "Wild boy."

"I know, I know you're a wild boy."

"Wild boy bad."

"No, you're not bad," I say. "Cracker Jack? Did something bad happen? What happened?"

"Mommy mad. I broke book." He takes some crumpled pages

from his pocket. They are pages from the picture book Dumpling was reading to him.

"Where is your mommy?" I ask. "Is she here? Is she okay?"

"Mommy mad. Wild boy run away."

"There's no fire?" I ask. "No one is dead?" Maybe I'm not too late. Maybe I can still get to them.

Cracker Jack scrunches his face. He looks confused. He repeats the word *dead*.

"Do you want to go home now?" I hold out my hand. Cracker Jack puts all five of his fingers in it. I clasp them.

Shadow leads us to the stake marker with the red dot, and through the woods to Hobo Town. It is just like I left it. Nothing destroyed. Nothing burned. Nothing smoldering. No ash. No death.

We get to Onion and Dumpling's tent. Dumpling is pacing and crying. She runs to Cracker Jack the second she sees us and engulfs him in her arms. "Darling, darling. I was so worried."

"Mommy mad," Cracker Jack says.

"No," Dumpling says. "Well, I *was* mad, but it doesn't mean I don't love you more than the sunshine, Cracker Jack." She kisses the top of his head. "It's just a book. We'll tape it back together. Okay, honey? Just don't run away like that. You scared us so much."

Onion appears and his haggard face instantly turns to joy at the sight of Cracker Jack. He kneels down and the three of them make a family huddle.

Finally they break apart. Cracker Jack's legs wrap around his mother's waist. He reaches his arms around his father's neck, so they are all still connected. Dumpling notices me standing there.

"You found him," she says.

"He was at the tracks," I explain.

Onion comes over and embraces me, whispering, "Thank you, thank you, thank you," over and over.

"What happened?" Dumpling asks. "We thought you'd made it onto the train for sure. We thought you'd be home by now."

"You have to leave," I say.

"What do you mean?" Onion asks, frowning.

I tell them about being chased by the rail bulls; about falling and thinking they'd killed Shadow, and what I'd overheard about their plan to burn down Hobo Town. "They would have killed me. It's serious. You have to leave."

Onion mutters under his breath, "I knew it. Newbies."

"I'm sorry," I say. "I'm really sorry. I know if they hadn't found me, this wouldn't have happened. It's all my fault."

Dumpling puts her hand on my shoulder. "It's not your fault, Blue. You didn't tell them. They've known we were here for eons. It was only a matter of time." She glares at Onion. "Onion knows that, too."

"Three years," Onion says. "That's a long stretch. We'll have to pack up and move on again." He gives me a wry smile, and his tone completely shifts. "We don't need half this shit we've collected in the last three years. Maybe it's a blessing to have to move."

Cracker Jack takes my hand and makes a song out of my name. Shadow nuzzles my other hand.

"Sure you don't want to come with us, Blue? Help us settle in a new town? Start all over?" Onion asks. "You're kind of one of us. Even if you need some train-hopping training."

I shake my head. "I have to go," I say. "I have to go home. I just came to warn you."

There is silence for a minute. Then Onion jumps up. "Well, then," he says. "We've got to rouse everyone and break down camp. You best head out."

"Where will you go?" I ask.

"Don't worry about us," Dumpling says. "We're tinkers. We'll find things. We'll fix things. We'll make a new home. We'll carry on."

"Bye, Boo!" Cracker Jack wraps his little arms around my leg.

Onion comes over. "Thanks for the warning." He puts his hand on my shoulder. "You're a survivor, like Snake said."

As I walk away I hear them waking everyone up, and the town begins to rustle with movement. They will be okay.

# Before

We moved. Five hundred miles west, five hundred miles from the coast, five hundred miles from home. We got there just as it was getting dark. The house was all one level, no winding staircase with a curved banister, no creaking, loose floorboard where I could hide things, no surf, no salty breeze, no seagulls. The rooms were big and barren and carpeted. Everything was clean and slick. The movers had already arrived, and boxes were stacked everywhere. All of our stuff stuffed into cardboard.

We'd been there less than an hour and Mom was already on her computer sitting in one of the unwrapped chairs at the kitchen breakfast bar, prepping for work.

"Where's all the sheets and stuff?" I asked. "I want to go to bed."

"I think the linen boxes are downstairs."

I found Dad in the basement-den, on his knees fiddling with some electric wires and mumbling to himself. He raised a hand when he saw me. "Whoever built this house didn't have his head on straight. It looks like these wires go right over the gas line. In the floor, of all places. This can't be up to code."

"This was a mistake," I said.

He frowned. "It's all right, sweetheart. Don't worry. I'll get someone in to rewire the whole place." He stood straight.

"No, I mean all of this. Moving. This house. I *hate* it here!" I grabbed a box labeled "Linen" and ran upstairs and shut the door on him. I wanted to hit something. Instead I just yelled. "I will *never* forgive you for making me move here. I want to go home!"

Dad followed me into the kitchen, where Mom looked up from her laptop. She gave him a warning glance, as if it was his responsibility to keep me quiet.

"You can't go back," my dad said.

"Why not?" I asked.

Mom sighed. "Please don't have a fit. We live here now. You only have one year of high school left. Then you'll be going to college."

"What if I don't want to go to college?" My voice rose.

Now both my parents sighed.

"Of course you're going to go to college," my mother said.

"Well, what if I don't get in? Did you ever think of that? What if you have to admit you have a stupid daughter?" It was true, my grades weren't more than average and my extracurricular activities were pathetic, to say the least.

Mom stood and closed her computer. "I know you're upset right now, but it will get better, sweetie, you'll see. This is still so new."

She tried to touch me, but I jerked away, accidentally hitting her arm as I did.

"You are out of your mind if you think I'm going to *stay* in this town one more second than I have to!" I yelled. "There's nothing to do here!"

"You didn't do anything in our old town, either." Now Mom's voice was rising. "You just sat around all day watching TV, eating crap food, and seeing that no-good boy behind our backs."

"That's not true! You don't know anything about my life!" I held up my wrist and pointed to the bracelet. "See this? He gave it to me. He loved me! He's the best thing that has ever happened to me." I ran down the long hallway to my new, ugly bedroom. I turned around and gave my parents one more outburst. "I wish you and this house would disappear!"

I slammed the door. I threw myself down on the mattress. We hadn't even set up the bed frame yet.

If I'd had anywhere to go, I would've snuck out and stayed there all night. I would have gone all the way back home if I could. I started to cry. I was fat and ugly and alone. I just wanted to be home. Maybe at first Jake had only asked me out on a bet, but in the end he liked me. He actually liked me. He said so.


The next morning I woke up early. There was no sound of gulls, no smell of ocean. It was hot and still. The weather here was supermuggy in the summer and supercold and snowy in the winter. Something about the effect of the valley and the lake. It was the absolute worst of both seasons.

I went to the kitchen to make coffee. I couldn't find the coffee machine or filters or anything in any of the boxes. Mom and Dad were still asleep. I threw on a pair of shorts and a sweatshirt, slid into my flip-flops. There must be a café or a convenience store or something where I could find a cup of coffee. I locked the door behind me and wandered out in search of caffeine.

# Now

I'm back on the road going east. Cars pass. An RV slows down and stops several yards ahead. When I reach it, a wrinkled, red-bearded man opens the door and steps down.

He asks, "You need a ride?"

I hesitate, not sure if he's safe.

"We're headed to the coast, if you want to hop along." He gestures for me to climb in.

I let Shadow sniff the guy to see if he gets the Shadow approval. He does, so I say okay. Shadow jumps into the RV before me. Inside, a woman is behind the wheel. She's got snow-white hair in a short cut.

"Howdy," she says. She puts her hand out for Shadow and pats his head. "I'm Ellen. This is Arthur."

"Thanks for the ride," I say.

"Make yourself at home." Arthur sits in the passenger seat and points to the back.

It's set up like a cozy living room with a couple of cushioned chairs, a table that folds out from the wall, a sink and mirror in the corner with some built-in cupboards over them. Long benches covered in padding and pillows stretch along the edge of the roof — room enough for four to sleep. I sit in one of the chairs.

"Where you headed?" Ellen asks.

"Home," I say. I am used to saying it now, even if it doesn't quite ring true.

She tips a pretend hat. "Home is good. We sold our house for this RV. Drove it south, lived there six months, and now we're heading back. We didn't fit in down there."

"In other words, I don't play golf," Arthur says.

"And I don't wear perfume," Ellen says. They continue with a back-and-forth routine, telling the story together.

Arthur: "And we actually missed the winters."

Ellen: "And the humidity made my hair go wonky."

Arthur: "And call me crazy, but I just don't like alligators."

Ellen: "Or brown recluse spiders."

Arthur: "Or the politics—but don't get me started on that."

Ellen: "This is our home now. We can go anywhere."

Arthur puts his hand on the top of Ellen's head. "Home is wherever you are, bunny rabbit."

Ellen blushes and rolls her eyes, but she smiles at the same time and touches his hand with her own. She turns to me. "Would you believe we've been together fifty years?"

"Best fifty years of my life." Arthur says. "You know what the secret is?" He faces me.

I shake my head.

"No kids," he says.

"Don't tell her that, Arthur. She's just a kid herself. She might *want* kids." Ellen turns around. "Don't listen to him. Plenty of couples with kids are completely happy."

"It wouldn't have been good for us," Arthur explains, although he's facing Ellen now. "We're artists. We're self-centered and pompous."

"Speak for yourself." She rolls her eyes again.

"Excuse me," Arthur says. "*I'm* self-centered and pompous. Ellen is an angel."

"Not exactly. I'm self-centered, too." Ellen smiles.

Arthur turns to me again. "You got parents?"

I don't know what to say. I do, don't I? Isn't that where I'm going? To see my parents? Tell them I'm sorry. And to see Jake? Find out if he really liked me. My heart beats fast as I nod my head slowly.

"Of course you do. Everyone's got parents, even if they're not around," Arthur says, matter of factly.

Ellen makes a clucking sound of annoyance. "Leave the poor girl alone."

"Sorry," he says to her, then to me, "Sorry. Didn't mean to pry."

They are quiet after that. Arthur puts in a CD and starts to hum. Soon they are both singing as if I weren't there. Their voices are soothing.

What did I know about my parents, really? Did they even love me? I guessed they did because I was their daughter and they had to. The same way I loved them because they were my parents. But was I an embarrassment to them? Was I someone who held them back from what they really wanted? My mother would have finished law school long ago if she hadn't had me. My father would have been able to futz around and do carpentry projects. Life would have been so much easier if I never existed in the first place.

I stare out the window at the pine trees on the side of the road. Someone like me could be hiding out there, surviving, living separate from the rest of the world. But perhaps it is not so separate after all. Snake, the people at Hobo Town, even Ellen and Arthur are laughing, crying, loving, working, moving, just the same as everyone else. They have joy and they have problems. They have life.

What was it I had loved about Jake? I can't remember. He seems so long ago in another time. I don't even remember who I was before now.

We drive past some cows in a field. They go by so fast. They don't talk to me. They don't notice me—why should they care about another vehicle passing? It happens all the time.

We take a ramp onto the highway, and I am in sudden culture shock. Cars come from all directions, whizzing by at high speed. Even though the RV is big and old, Ellen keeps up with the traffic. It feels like the world is spinning out of control. Who can be in the moment when everything is headed so fast to get somewhere in the future? What will be there when I get home?

*All dead. All dead.* Who is all dead?

I concentrate on Ellen and Arthur singing, the steady whir of traffic and the occasional honking of car horns. I concentrate on staying awake, but my eyelids are so heavy I have to close them for a minute.

I see my yellow house. I see my parents waiting for me in the doorway like they used to when I came home from elementary school. They look different. They look happy. They walk down the driveway. My father opens his arms ready to embrace me. My mother quickens her pace. When they are only a few steps away, my father stretches out his hand to touch me, my mother reaches to kiss me. But right before they get to me, in a sudden instant, they wither and crumble to the ground. Their bodies are gone and there is only smoke and dust. Some of the dust lies in a pile at my feet; some drifts into the wind.

*No one survived. All dead. All dead.*

Deafening. Suffocating. I scream for help. *Snake!*

A hand touches my shoulder.

I open my eyes. The RV has stopped on the side of the highway. It is morning. Arthur is kneeling in front of me, shaking me gently. "You've been asleep for hours. Were you having a nightmare?"

Shadow whimpers at my other side and licks my hand. I reach out and rub his ears. "I . . . I think so," I say.

"Was it about snakes?" Ellen stands above me looking worried. "You were yelling a word. It sounded like *snake*."

"I know someone named Snake," I say. "He must have been there—in my dream." I shake myself fully awake. "I'm okay."

"Are you sure?" Ellen asks. She hands me a glass of water, which I drink readily.

"Yeah. I just need to get home. Where are we?"

They tell me the name of a town I recognize.

"I'm almost there," I say. "I can walk the rest of the way."

"Are you sure?" Ellen says again. "It doesn't seem right to just drop you off after a nightmare. We can take you."

"It's okay," I say in my most convincing voice. "I want to walk. I have to."

Arthur nods as though he understands. "I can't imagine you want to be dropped off by a couple of old wackos in an ancient RV." He turns to Ellen. "We'll probably cause more trouble for her. Not to mention embarrassment."

Ellen sighs. "Okay. But if something happens, promise you'll go to the police?"

I nod, even though it's a lie. "I have Shadow. He protects me."

Gulls circle overhead. I smell the ocean. Shadow does, too. His nostrils twitch in the salty air.

I should be excited, but I am shaking and nervous. Eudora said I would remember everything when I was ready. "Am I ready?" I whisper. Shadow leans into me and I take a minute to massage his back.

I will go to Jake's first. His house is before mine. After all, he is one of the people I want to see. Right? But as I turn down his street I wonder. When I try to remember his face, I see Snake. When I try to remember his touch, I feel Snake.

Jake's red sports car is parked in front of his house. It's the same car, polished squeaky clean. The top is down. There are two people sitting in it. Jake and a girl. Jake leans toward her, and their heads mush together. They are making out. I know I shouldn't be watching this, but I can't help it. I know it should be bothering me, but it doesn't. Not really. I don't feel anything. Shadow sits on my foot as if trying to keep me in place.

They break apart and Jake gets out. I can see him better now. He is wearing a tight T-shirt showing off more muscles than I remember. His hair is perfect, copper, and slick. He looks the same, but is he? Has he always been this clean-cut? Has he always looked this superficial? He's not even that handsome. The way he swaggers around his car to open the passenger door makes him seem pompous. I remember his glistening smile, his perfectly straight teeth. I was totally sucked in by that smile. I was sucked in by all the things he said to me. I didn't even hear the shallowness underneath. Is it possible that I was that shallow myself? I remember what Adrianna said—Jake is not all he is cracked up to be.

The girl in the passenger seat gets out. A thin, pretty, perfect girl. Someone who would be in the elite crowd for sure. But then, maybe she's not what she's cracked up to be, either.

Jake walks behind the girl, his eyes glued to her butt. Then he catches up to her and puts his arm around her. The girl flips her hair. She is totally in love with him. For a second I consider yelling out to her not to get sucked in, but before I can do anything, Jake bends over and kisses her and they go inside.

Jake is the same. But I am not. He never loved me. And more important, I never loved him.

I need to go home now more than ever. See my mother and my father. I have to tell them I am sorry for everything, tell them I love them. I have to make sure they're okay.

But there is one person I have to call first. I take the phone card and the Overlook Motel card from my pocket.

I turn my back on Jake and walk away, with Shadow at my heels.

There is a pay phone outside Joe's One-Stop. I punch in all the numbers. My heart is racing.

"Good morning. Overlook." It is Snake's squirrelly voice, professional and cheerful. "May I help you?"

"Hi," I say.

"Oh, hey!" He recognizes me. "Are you okay?"

"I think so."

"That's good," he says.

I tell him about Hobo Town and the rail bulls, and how they got out in time. "It won't be there if you go back. I don't know where they went."

"They can take care of themselves," he says. "It's what they're good at."

"But the bulls wouldn't have known if it weren't for me," I say.

"That's not true," Snake insists. "You saved them." I hear yipping in the background.

"How's Pity?" I ask.

"She's a handful. She's chewing on my shoelace right now."

"She'll grow out of it."

"How's Shadow?"

I touch the tips of Shadow's pointy ears. "He's good," I say.

There is an awkward silence. The phone feels cold in my hand. Suddenly I am shivering. I want to say things, but I can't.

"It's nice to hear from you," Snake says. "I wasn't sure I would."

"I wanted to let you know I got here. And I wanted to tell you about Hobo Town." Pause. "And to thank you for"—I feel the robot clock he made for me, still in my pocket—"for the clock . . . and everything."

"You're welcome," he says.

I nod, even though he can't see me. "Listen, about that other guy . . ." I take a deep breath, then go on. "It's nothing. I remembered him all wrong."

"That happens," he says.

I want to say it is okay. That everything is okay. That Snake is who I want, but it's not quite right to say all this. There's too much else in my head, and Snake is not part of all that. I don't trust my feelings, and I don't trust my memory. Not yet.

The phone clicks the warning sign that the card is almost out of time. "I have to go," I say.

"Blue?" Snake says.

"Yeah?"

"No one can do it all by themselves. People want to help. Let them."

The phone goes dead. Maybe Snake and I will see each other again. If we do, I want to be sure I am me.


I walk down the street, turn left. There is my house at the top of the hill. It's still pale yellow with green shutters. There's a car in the driveway. Not my parents' car. There is an upside-down kiddie pool in the yard—we never had one of those—and a tricycle with pink tassels on the handlebars. I start running, and as I get closer I notice the window curtains are different, too. Something is amiss.

Is it my house? Did I end up at the wrong place? My pulse quickens.

I hide behind the maple tree near a freshly raked pile of leaves and stare at the front door. I half expect to see myself come out. But something deep down tells me that I no longer live here, that my life will never be the same.

I imagine opening the front door and walking up the steps, holding on to the curved railing, entering the first room at the top. My room. Surely there must be something of me still in there.

Is the tree mural still on the wall? Is there a candy bar still under the floorboard? If not, then there is nothing of me left anywhere. Having something of me still in this house is the only hope I have of proving that I exist.

I touch Shadow. I look into his eyes and wait for him to say something. He whimpers and I realize I haven't heard him speak for a while. "What?" I ask. He barks once. His bark seems to tell me something. He is with me, but I am on my own. "I love you," I tell him.

The front door of my house opens and a little girl in a purple tutu and white sneakers flies out. Her braids bounce as she twirls across the yard.

Before I can stop him, Shadow darts over to her and wags his tail superfast. The girl stops still. Her mouth spreads in a huge, goofy grin, and she starts bouncing up and down on one leg. She puts her hand out for Shadow to sniff, which he does, and then she pat-pats him on the top of his head.

"Hello," she says to him. "I was just wishing for a dog. Are you a magic dog? Can you do tricks?"

Shadow stands on his hind legs. The girl claps. Shadow dances backwards, leading her to the tree. The girl follows him until she stops directly in front of me. She stares up and down.

"Are you a fairy godmother?" she finally asks with wide eyes.

I look down at my filthy clothes. My hair is matted and I probably smell like garbage. "I don't think so," I say.

"Are you a witch, then?"

"No."

She stares at me with great seriousness, then breaks into sudden joy and exclaims, "I remember you!" She claps her hands together. "How did you get here? Didn't you move far away? Did your magic dog bring you here?"

"I don't know," I answer, looking at Shadow. "Maybe he did."

"He *is* magic," the girl says with assurance. Shadow darts around her.

"You may be right," I say.

"I'm Sophie," the girl says. "I live here." From inside my house, her house now, a woman's face appears in the window. "With my mom and dad, and baby brother."

"I used to live here," I say.

She nods. "Yes, I know. We met in the bedroom with the trees. I finished painting the little house for the ghosts. I hope you don't mind."

"I don't mind," I say.

"There are ghosts living in it, I'm sure of it. And they're friendly ghosts, not scary at all. Where do *you* live now?" she asks.

The woman in the window moves away. The front door opens, and she comes toward us. She's wearing an apron like she's just been baking. She is smiling but she looks worried, too.

I step behind the tree. "I don't live anywhere," I say. "We moved far away. The new house blew up. My parents are dead. Everything is gone. No one survived. All dead." This slips out of me as if I've known all along. It is my voice, but it sounds different, as though it is coming from somewhere and someone else. But at the same time I know that it is me who is speaking these words.

Sophie's eyes open even wider and her jaw drops. "But . . ." She sniffles. "But . . . *you're* not dead." Her face crumples and she begins to cry.

I didn't mean to upset her. I want to tell her everything is okay, that it doesn't matter. I finger the robot clock in my pocket. I take it out and give it to Sophie.

She stops crying and examines it.

"Someone special gave this to me," I tell her, "but I want you to take care of it. Can you do that?"

She nods with her mouth open.

Beyond her I see the woman, her mother, getting closer—I can't explain this to her; I can't explain it to anyone. A wave of blackness overtakes me. All that I have said, I realize, is the truth.

I am the missing girl. My parents are dead.

I am the one who survived.

# Now and Before

I am aware of Sophie yelling. I am aware of Shadow barking. I am aware of the kind woman telling me to wait. My head is spinning and all sounds fade away as I run, until there is only silence and the wind in my face.

There is only me.

I see clearly what happened. I was so mad at my parents. They made me move to that stupid town and that ugly house, as though I were irrelevant. I hated that house and that town and them.

Yet, I knew I didn't *really* hate them. I didn't wish everything gone. It was a fluke. A random act of destruction. Might I have prevented it, though? Or would I have died along with them? How come I lived and they didn't? I should have been asleep in my bed. I should be dead. It's their fault that I am alive.

That morning I went out to find coffee. I was heading home when there was a loud boom. I thought it was an earthquake. As I got closer I could smell the gas and burning ash. Smoke permeated my nostrils, making me dizzy. I ran faster. As I rounded the corner, I saw commotion at the top of the hill where the house had stood, where my parents had been sleeping in their new bedroom surrounded by boxes filled with everything we owned.

There was a scene: fire trucks, police cars, an ambulance. There were strangers: screaming, watching, and pointing to the pile of rubble and timber that used to be a house. Some of the houses around were damaged, but this one was gone. The firemen were trying to put out fires that had started. The sky was filled with smoke and the smell of burning ash.

The police were trying to keep people back. Their faces were covered with masks, and they were handing out masks to the strangers. "It's not safe," they said. "The gas will make you sick. Put these on."

I crept closer without anyone noticing. I crouched behind a fire truck. The smoke made my eyes sting. The smell made me want to throw up. I saw the door of our refrigerator sticking up from the rubble and a bedspring next to it. The bed my mother had been sleeping on? I thought I saw a part of her. A part of my mother's body. I couldn't identify anything else.

I stood frozen on the edge of chaos. Something in me left— rose up to the sky to mix with the ash and smoke. What stayed on the ground was someone else. This was not my home. It had never been and never would be. Home was far, far away, with the smell of the ocean and the sound of the gulls, and my parents alive and a boy who I believed loved me, at least liked me. Not this smoky, crumpled mess of death.

I heard a cop talking to one of the firemen. "Could anyone have survived?"

The fireman answered, "No, no one can survive this kind of explosion. We'll know for sure when we find all the bodies."

I moved away. I heard the neighbors, all strangers to me, talking.

"What happened?"

"A gas leak."

"It's a tragedy."

"It's freaky."

"Thank God our house is old and solid."

"Those new homes went up so fast."

"There's a lawsuit here for sure."

"Who's going to sue? That family just moved in. They had a daughter."

"No one survived. They're all dead."

No one knew me in that town. They thought I was dead. It made no sense. I wasn't dead. I didn't live there. So I ran. I left the scene and I went back home.

Where I am now.

But now that I am here I see my old house and I know. I know it isn't mine anymore. I know we moved. I know the new house is gone. I know my parents are gone. I've come five hundred miles, and now I know. Everything is gone.

This time when I run, I am running to the ocean. I will not stop until I have no breath left. There is nothing to save me. I do not want to be a survivor.

. . .

I hear the surf. My heart races. The vast expanse of ocean opens in front of me—it goes on and on, forever and ever, mysterious and inviting, frightening and comforting all at the same time.

I run to the beach, stop for a second to take off my shoes, and burrow my toes in the pebbly sand.

I step into the water. It's freezing.

I take another step, then another and another. I don't need to run anymore.

The water reaches my thighs.

I keep going.

The water reaches my waist.

I keep going.

Tingles of icy cold water reach my armpits, then my neck and chin. The salty taste creeps into my mouth.

I keep going.

This is where I was headed all along—deep in the icy waters of nothingness.

The ocean covers all of me, enveloping me. It's not cold anymore. In fact, it's warm. It's my mother's and my father's arms wrapped around me in a sandwich hug.

"Welcome home," my mother says.

And then my father, "We knew you'd make it."

They are under water but their voices are crystal clear.

"I'm sorry," I whisper. My words come out muffled and leave a trail of bubbles.

They squeeze me tight. "It's not your fault," they say. "We're sorry, too." Their grip intensifies until it starts to hurt, and it's hard to breathe.

From far away I hear the sound of a dog barking. I try to tell my parents to let go, but when I open my mouth it fills with salty water and I cough and swallow more water. I struggle to unwrap their arms but it's like they are an anchor, holding me down.

Something breaks the surface above me and I see four submerged paws doggy-paddling. I pull with all my might and manage to get my head out of the water even though my parents keep hold.

"Let me go!" My voice erupts into the waves. But I only get air for a second before I am sucked under again. I look for my parents, but there is only a mass of seaweed spiraling around my legs and body, gripping me tight, pulling me down.

I kick frantically, trying to untangle myself. Shadow is near, paddling like crazy. He dives underneath and bites through the seaweed, and I am released.

The sun hits my face. I hear the whir of a motorboat. A child's voice shouts: "There she is! Save her!"

I put my head below the ocean once more. My parents are there again. They are not strangling me. They are floating away from me. This is my last chance.

"Wait!" I scream, choking the words out. "Can I come with you?"

They turn. My mother's sad eyes sparkle in the sea light. She whispers, "Darling. No."

My father smiles and shakes his head. "You have to stay."

"But how? What do I do?"

"You live," my mother says.

"Be brave. People will help," my father says.

"But who?" I plead, using the last reserve of air left in my lungs. I have so much to ask before they go, but I can't.

They reach out. I reach out. Our hands touch.

"You'll know. You already know," they say as they slowly drift away. Eventually just the tips of our fingers are connected. Then our fingertips part, and they float into the darkness of the sea and I can't see them anymore. They are gone.

Shadow circles around me in the water. My parents are right. I *do* know. I know Shadow has come to rescue me. I know I have to go on. For some reason, with some random stroke of luck, good or bad, I survived and they did not.

I grab on to Shadow's neck and he paddles me to the boat. Arms outstretch and I am hoisted up. Shadow is hoisted up, too. A towel is draped over me, and I huddle, clutching Shadow in my arms.

Over the wind and the surf I hear my parents' voices carry through the waters. They are calling my name. First it is the name they gave me, then it changes to "Blue." Their voices get softer and softer until all I can make out is the chant of one word: "Live. Live. Live."

# ACKNOWLEDGMENTS

My thanks to all the good people at Houghton Mifflin Harcourt, especially Margaret Wimberger, Susanna Vagt, and my amazing editor, Julia Richardson; to Lisa Bowe, Louise Hawes, Mary Logue, and Pam Richards for friendship, support, and feedback on various drafts; to Julia Ackerman, LCSW, for providing information on acute stress disorder and other accuracy checks; to Kyle and Sophie Richards-Connolly for being the awesome young adults in my life; to my mother, Elena, and brother, Eric, for the creative and courageous lives they lead, and to the memory of my father, Garrett; and Ed Briant for our ongoing conversations about everything under the sun.

A special thanks to the woman I met ten years ago who lost everything and who shared her story with me. And thanks to the trainhoppers and travelers I've encountered along the way. May you all find your true home.

And, of course, extra pats to Happy and Rico for their inimitably divine dogginess.